UNCLE REMUS

UNCLE REMUS

JOEL CHANDLER HARRIS

Illustrations by A. B. Frost

Introduction by Stella Brewer Brookes

SCHOCKEN BOOKS · NEW YORK

First published 1880

First SCHOCKEN edition 1965

10 9 8   81 82 83 84

Copyright © 1965 by Schocken Books

Library of Congress Catalog Card No. 65-14828

Manufactured in the United States of America

ISBN 0-8052-0101-7 paperback
ISBN 0-8052-3273-7 hardcover

CONTENTS

CONTENTS.

INTRODUCTION

AMONG the immortal "real folks" of literature Uncle
Remus' place is secure; in the ancient order of story-
tellers his fame is international. This figure which Joel
Chandler Harris added to the gallery of world portraits
is as much a part of literature as Rip Van Winkle or the
inimitable Micawber. What Harris gave to literature was
not a Character but a Portrait. Uncle Remus is an indi-
vidual—a distinctive personality. Harris' aim was not to
give the picture of an entire race; what he did was to
choose from that race a dramatic human figure that appealed to him as picturesque and moving. It is true that
he used the plantation as the background against which
the old man's figure is silhouetted, for character cannot
exist independent of a setting. Yet Uncle Remus emerges
from his background as a genius in the art of storytelling
and there are few, either in fiction or real life, who can
reach his stature. Storytelling is an art and Uncle Remus
is an artist.

The pattern of the tales was an innovation recognized by all readers of stories. Though Harris said, ''There is nothing here but an old negro man, a little boy, and a dull reporter,'' one realizes that the strong frame in which his portraits were placed is an artistic conception. He opens the first book with a picture of the old man and the little boy which remains constant throughout nine of the books. Although, in later books, the boy grows up and a son takes his place with Uncle Remus, the structure of child and storyteller remains the same and gives shape to the work.

Harris uses the dramatic monologue as a principal means of character revelation, though brief descriptions of the old man interpolated throughout the stories add to the graphic presentation. The dramatic monologue was certainly no new form in literature, but Harris put it to new uses, aided by his unrivaled power of language and his accurate knowledge of folk speech. What makes Uncle Remus so true to life is that Harris captured not only what the old man said, but his manner of saying it. To transfer gesture to the printed page is indeed difficult, and these are the touches that elevate Harris' character to originality and establish his reputation as a master in the creation of atmosphere and, specifically, the creation of a character who breathes. The venerable fabulist was apparently Harris' embodiment of the aim stated in the Introduction to his first book, ''. . . to present the pic-

turesque sensitiveness—a curious exaltation of mind and
temperament, not to be defined by words."

Uncle Remus was not the first plantation storyteller in
fiction; but none had so completely revealed himself as
did he. Herein lies the essence of Harris' art: one is con-
vinced after reading the ten books of the careful delinea-
tion of the man. Harris reveals Uncle Remus' method:
"He liked to be asked for a story so that he might have
an opportunity of indulging in a friendly dispute, a
wrangle of words, and then suddenly end it all by telling
the tale that happened to be on his mind at the moment.
In short, he delighted to whet the expectations of the
youngster, and arouse his enthusiasm."

Various are the roles which Uncle Remus plays. Sometimes he scourges mischief: "I boun' I ain't gwine ter fix
you no mo' contraptions, ef dat's de way you does—
massycreein' de cats, en de Dominicker chickens, en de
Lord knows what! Ef you er huntin' war, des go up
yonder whar dat ar Dominicker hen got de young chickens; go up dar en 'sturb her, en ef she don't make you
squall, de first letter er my name ain't Remus."[1]

Uncle Remus' method of quarreling with the little boy
was inimitable. The youngster had learned to be obedient
if he wanted the story finished. For example:

> "Well, honey," said the old man, wiping his spec-
> tacles, "hit sorter runs dis away: One time dey wuz a
> man w'at had a mightly likely daughter."

"Was he a white man or a black man?" the little boy asked.

"I 'clar to gracious, honey!" exclaimed the old man, "you er pushin' me mos' too close. Fer all I ken tell you, de man mount er bin ez w'ite ez de driven snow, er he mout er bin de blackes' Affi'kin er de whole kit en bilin'. I'm des tellin' you de tale, en you kin take de man en w'itewash 'im, er you kin black 'im up des ez you please. Dat's de way I looks at it."[2]

At another time he cautions the little boy about his choice of friends: "I dunner w'at in der name er goodness you wanter be copyin' atter dem ar Favereses fer. Ef youer gwine ter copy atter yuther folks, copy atter dem w'at some 'count.'"[3] Sometimes he is a philosopher. One day when he and the little boy are talking over things in general, he remarks:

'T'ain't de biggest en de strongest dat does de mostest in dis world. . . . No, honey, don't let nobody fool you 'bout dat. De cuckle-burr got needer life ner lim', yit when it gits in de sheep wool it kin travel fast ez de sheep, you know dat . . . de ole elephen' may be strong, en de tiger may be servigrous . . . but Brer Rabbit done outdone um.[4]

He indulges in aphorisms, shrewd observations, curious retorts, homely thrusts—all of which become a commentary on life. Sometimes the criticism takes a pungent turn; often one notices a felicity of phrase abounding in similes and metaphors; frequently there is a poetic release where his words move with rhythm and flow with eloquence. Note how he describes old times, ". . . way back yonder when de clouds wuz thicker dan what dey is now, an' when de sun ain't had ter go to bed at night ter keep fum being tired de next day."[5] He delighted in mouth filling, many-syllabled words, some of which seem nonsensical, but which appealed to him because of their sonority. Uncle Remus also talks of gossip, "De word went 'roun' an' when it came back ter whar it started, it ain't look like itse'f." He knows something of the gossip monger, too: "She had a tongue wid salt en pepper on it."

The author always retires behind the scene and allows the wise, genial old man not only to tell the stories but also to express psychological and philosophical reactions to the world in which he lives. Upon the inquiry of an interviewer as to who suggested the character, Harris replied that he was not an invention of his own but a human composite of three or four old Negroes whom he had just "walloped together."[6] So distinct a personality as Uncle Remus may never again be chronicled. His naive drollery, his whimsical incongruities, his aphorisms, quaintly expressed—all peculiar to himself—make up his character. He caught them from no one and to no one has he imparted them.

Some literary historians declare that American folklore began with Uncle Remus. Although one may not be able to accept so sweeping a verdict, for in a sense Franklin and Irving were folklorists, the claim for Harris is authentic enough to afford a convenient introduction to his work. It seems safe to speculate that the Uncle Remus stories, published in 1880, if not the first of this distinctive type of literature, were at least prominently the means of creating a vogue which swept the country in the early 1880's. Harris called himself an "accidental author"; his surprise at the flood of inquiries which came to him mark him as also an "accidental folklorist." The numerous letters which he received with regard to this element in his stories first amazed, then amused, but finally aroused and interested him. When by December 8, 1880, the first Uncle Remus book had passed through its fourth edition, it had been noticed by every paper of importance in the country. Scientific journals devoted columns to it as a contribution to folklore.

After Harris' interest had been aroused in the subject, he persistently held that his stories were "uncooked"— that they were "pure folklore." The stories that appeared in the first book bear greater evidence of pure folklore than those which appeared in subsequent books. Perhaps the most convincing evidence offered in proof of the folklore element throughout the series is the inclusion in many of the stories of "Miss Meadows an' de gals." Of this subtle, whimsical creation—so intimately a part of the stories and existing in natural relationship with the animal creatures—Harris seems to have had no definite conception. The illustrations for the first edition of *Uncle Remus: His Songs and His Sayings* were to be done by Frederick Church and James Moser. Mr. Church, puzzled as to what he should do with "Miss Meadows an' de gals," wrote Harris: "What is your idea of 'Miss Meadows an' de gals'? . . . perhaps they just mean *Nature,* in which case I should depict them as pretty girls in simple costumes, making a charming contrast to the ludicrous positions of the animals."[7]

Mr. Harris seemed pleased with the suggestion, but he reemphasized the idea that he was only the "compiler" of the stories. He wrote, "My relations to the sketches you are illustrating are those of compiler merely; consequently I cannot pretend to know what is meant by Miss Meadows . . . Why she is there, I cannot say, but your conception will give the sketches a poetical color (if I may say so) which will add vastly to whatever interest they may have for people of taste. By all means let Miss Meadows figure as Nature in the shape of a beautiful girl in a simple but not unpicturesque costume. As it is your own conception, I know you will treat the young lady tenderly . . ."[8] The same "conception" of "Miss Meadows an' de gals" occurred to Rudyard Kipling.

Harris had written an appreciation of Kipling's *Jungle Book* and Kipling wrote a letter of thanks to Harris. At the conclusion of the letter, dated December 6, 1895, we find : "One thing I want to know badly (you must loathe the people who pester you with this kind of thing), but from what nature-myth or *what* come 'Miss Meadows and the girls?' Where do they begin—in whose mind? what do you think they are?"[9] In "Mr. Rabbit Deceives Mr. Fox," we come closest to an answer of sorts from Harris. When the Little Boy asks Uncle Remus "Who was Miss Meadows?" the storyteller answers "Don't ax me, honey. She wuz in de tale, Miss Meadows en de gals wuz, en de tale I give you like h'it wer' gun ter me."[10] It seems as if that was intended to end the inquiry.

It is significant that the Uncle Remus sketches began appearing in the columns of *The Atlanta Constitution* as early as 1878, and that the Tar-Baby story (which was extremely popular at home and abroad) appeared in 1879. Evidently Harris received many letters with regard to the folklore element in stories that appeared prior to publication of the first book in 1880. In his Introduction to this book he refers to the correspondence and tells his amazement at the interest manifested in this particular phase of the tales. In the same Introduction, he tells of his method of collecting, of variants of the stories included in the volume, and insists that his aim is to preserve the stories in their "original simplicity."

Despite his persistent refusal to acknowledge his art, Harris' correspondence and the productions themselves point to the fact that he did have skill and that he did consciously develop the art of writing through self-discipline. To discover this one has only to examine one of the "uncooked" stories sent to him by a Negro correspondent and compare it with the finished version. An exact report of a correspondent from Senoia, Georgia, was:

> Mr. Harris I have one tale of Uncle Remus that I have not seen in print yet. Bro Rabbit at Mis Meadows and Bro Bare went to Bro Rabbit house and eat up his children and set his house on fire and make like the children all burnt up but Bro Rabbit saw his track he knowed Bro Bare was the man so one day Bro Rabbit saw Bro Bare in the woods with his ax hunting a bee tree after Bro Rabbit spon howdy he tell Bro Bare he know where a bee tree was and he would go and show and help him cut it down they went and cut it an Bro Rabbit drove in the glut (wedge) while Bro Bare push his head in the hole Bro Rabbit nock out the glut and cut him hikry. Mr. Harris you have the tale now give it wit I never had room to give you all you can finish it.

This tale was the source of the story which appears in *Uncle Remus* under the title "The End of Mr. Bear."[12]

One of the best appraisals in connection with the respective literary and folklore elements is that given by Mark Twain. On August 4, 1881, Harris had written in a letter to Mark Twain:

> Everybody has been kind to the old man, but you have been the kindest of all. I am perfectly aware that my book has no basis of literary art to stand upon; I know it is the matter and not the manner that has attracted public attention and won the consideration of people of taste in the North; I understand that my relations toward Uncle Remus are similar to those that exist between an almanac-maker and the calendar; but at the same time I feel grateful to those who have taken the old man under their wing.[13]

Mark Twain realized his friend's modest valuation of his talents, and in his reply stated:

> You can argue yourself into the delusion that the principle of life is in the stories themselves and not in their setting, but you will save labor by stopping with that solitary convert, for he is the only intelligent one you will bag. In reality the stories are only alligator pears—one eats them merely for the sake of the dressing. "Uncle Remus" is most deftly drawn and is a lovable and delightful creation; he and the little boy and their relations with each other are bright, fine literature, and worthy to live...[14]

The Uncle Remus stories came into the world as a novelty, a genre not readily classifiable. To the North, they were a revelation of the unknown; to the South, they were an eye-opener to the charm of the familiar. To most Americans, the chief ingredient was humor. It was a new kind of humor in the history of American literature. Coming from a race good natured in the face of affliction, there was a propinquity of smiling and weeping, a wit which grew out of the fact that the ability to make an owner smile often saved a harsh lash. Harris wrote in the introduction to his first book:

> I am advised by my publishers that this book is to be included in their catalogue of humorous publications, and this friendly warning gives me an opportunity to say that however humorous it may be in effect, its intention is perfectly serious; and, even if it were otherwise, it seems to me that a volume written wholly in dialect must have its solemn, not to say melancholy, features.[15]

Aside from humor, the outstanding element was characterization—and characterization here means chiefly the creation of Uncle Remus. Harris once said, ''What does a story matter, if we do not, somehow, find its characters close kin to us?''[16]

The first Uncle Remus book was published in 1880, although the title page gives the year 1881. The 1880 edition was illustrated by F. S. Church and J. H. Moser. Harris was not pleased with the illustrations here, especially those of the animals. In 1895, a second edition appeared, with the illustrations by A. B. Frost which are reproduced in this volume. The author was ecstatic in his response and appreciation. *Nights With Uncle Remus: Myths and Legends of the Old Plantation* appeared in 1883. This was the second in the long series of Uncle Remus books. The third, *Daddy Jake the Runaway and Short Stories Told After Dark,* was published in 1889. In chronological order, the next book was *Uncle Remus and His Friends*, which appeared in 1892. Here Uncle Remus took a bow and formally announced his intention of retiring from story-telling. However, the old man did not succeed in giving up his audience and, by 1918, nine Uncle Remus books had appeared, the last published after Harris' death. The tenth Uncle Remus book was published in 1948, and presented manuscripts which, for one reason or another, had not been included in the earlier books.

The ten Uncle Remus books, although varying in a few aspects, have the same substance and the same philosophy. Harris had the genius to preserve the legends which he had imbibed during his youth, as well as the gift of vivid characterization. As a result, Uncle Remus is one of the great products of American literature. The immediate and wide-spread success of the first books projected their author before readers in every part of America, and in some foreign countries. Surely, Harris' talents carried him beyond his own modest intent: "As

I wrote them with my own children around me . . . or not far away, I seemed to see other children laughing as the homely stories were read to them; I seemed to see gray-haired children smiling, as if they found here, close to earth, a stroke of simplicity ringing true to life; and it seemed to me that these visions, vain though they might be, were more promising than a hopeless journey through the wilderness to discover at what hour the tribes of the mountains and citizens of the plains shook their hairy fists at each other and went jabbering their several ways."[17]

STELLA BREWER BROOKES

Clark College
Atlanta, Georgia

NOTES

With the kind permission of the University of Georgia Press and the author, the present introduction has been drawn from *Joel Chandler Harris—Folklorist* by Stella Brewer Brookes, copyright 1950 by the University of Georgia Press.

1. *Uncle Remus and His Friends,* Boston, 1892, p. 91.
2. *Daddy Jake the Runaway and Short Stories Told After Dark,* New York, 1889, pp. 171-172.
3. *Nights With Uncle Remus,* Boston, 1883, p. 17.
4. *Uncle Remus and His Friends,* p. 101.

5. *Uncle Remus Returns,* Boston, 1918, p. 134.
6. Julia Collier Harris remarks that Mr. J. T. Manry who worked on the *Monroe Advertiser* at Forsyth, Georgia, was of the opinion that the name Uncle Remus was a souvenir of Forsyth days. "The town gardener . . . was called Uncle Remus and Mr. Manry recalls that the name appealed to father's imagination at that time." See *The Life and Letters of Joel Chandler Harris,* by Julia Collier Harris, Boston and New York, 1918, p. 146.
7. *Life and Letters,* p. 149.
8. *Ibid.,* p. 150.
9. *Ibid.,* p. 334.
10. See p. 25.
11. *Life and Letters,* p. 197.
12. See p. 135.
13. *Life and Letters,* p. 168.
14. *Ibid.,* pp. 169-170.
15. *Uncle Remus: His Songs and His Sayings,* New York, 1880, p. vii.
16. *Life and Letters,* p. 570.
17. *Uncle Remus and His Friends,* p. vii.

UNCLE REMUS

UNCLE REMUS INITIATES THE LITTLE BOY.

ONE even-
ing recently,
the lady whom
Uncle Remus
calls "Miss
Sally" missed
her little sev-
en - year - old
boy. Making
search   for

him through the house and
through the yard, she heard
the sound of voices in the
old man's cabin, and, looking   through   the   window,
saw the child sitting by
Uncle Remus.   His head
rested against the old man's
arm, and he was gazing with an expression of the
most intense interest into the rough, weather-beaten

face, that beamed so kindly upon him. This is what " Miss Sally " heard :

" Bimeby, one day, arter Brer Fox bin doin' all dat he could fer ter ketch Brer Rabbit, en Brer Rabbit bin doin' all he could fer to keep 'im fum it, Brer Fox say to hisse'f dat he'd put up a game on Brer Rabbit, en he ain't mo'n got de wuds out'n his mouf twel Brer Rabbit come a lopin' up de big road, lookin' des ez plump, en ez fat, en ez sassy ez a Moggin hoss in a barley-patch.

" ' Hol' on dar, Brer Rabbit,' sez Brer Fox, sezee.

" ' I ain't got time, Brer Fox,' sez Brer Rabbit, sezee, sorter mendin' his licks.

" ' I wanter have some confab wid you, Brer Rabbit,' sez Brer Foz, sezee.

" ' All right, Brer Fox, but you better holler fum whar you stan'. I'm monstus full er fleas dis mawnin',' sez Brer Rabbit, sezee.

" ' I seed Brer B'ar yistiddy,' sez Brer Fox, sezee, ' en he sorter rake me over de coals kaze you en me ain't make frens en live naberly, en I told 'im dat. I'd see you.'

" Den Brer Rabbit scratch one year wid his off hinefoot sorter jub'usly, en den he ups en sez, sezee :

" ' All a settin', Brer Fox. Spose'n you drap roun' ter-morrer en take dinner wid me. We ain't got no great doin's at our house, but I speck de old 'oman en de chilluns kin sorter scramble roun' en git up sump'n fer ter stay yo' stummuck.'

"'I'm 'gree'ble, Brer Rabbit,' sez Brer Fox, sezee.

"'Den I'll 'pen' on you,' sez Brer Rabbit, sezee.

"Nex' day, Mr. Rabbit an' Miss Rabbit got up soon, 'fo' day, en raided on a gyarden like Miss Sally's out dar, en got some cabbiges, en some roas'n years, en some sparrer-grass, en dey fix up a smashin' dinner. Bimeby one er de little Rabbits, playin' out in de back-yard, come runnin' in hollerin', 'Oh, ma! oh, ma! I seed Mr. Fox a comin'!' En den Brer Rabbit he tuck de chilluns by der years en make um set down, en den him and Miss Rabbit sorter dally roun' waitin' for Brer Fox. En dey keep on waitin', but no Brer Fox ain't come. Atter 'while Brer Rabbit goes to de do', easy like, en peep out, en dar, stickin' fum behime de cornder, wuz de tip-een' er Brer Fox tail. Den Brer Rabbit shot de do' en sot down, en put his paws behime his years en begin fer ter sing :

> "'De place wharbouts you spill de grease,
>   Right dar youer boun' ter slide,
> An' whar you fine a bunch er ha'r,
>   You'll sholy fine de hide.'

"Nex' day, Brer Fox sont word by Mr. Mink, en skuze hisse'f kaze he wuz too sick fer ter come, en he ax Brer Rabbit fer to come en take dinner wid him, en Brer Rabbit say he wuz 'gree'ble.

" Bimeby, w'en de shadders wuz at der shortes',
Brer Rabbit he sorter brush up en santer down ter Brer
Fox's house, en w'en he got dar, he hear somebody
groanin', en. he look in de do' en dar he see Brer Fox
settin' up in a rockin' cheer all wrop up wid flannil, en
he look mighty weak. Brer Rabbit look all 'roun', he
did, but he ain't see no dinner. De dish-pan wuz settin' on de table, en close by wuz a kyarvin' knife.

" ' Look like you gwineter have chicken fer dinner,
Brer Fox,' sez Brer Rabbit, sezee.

" Yes, Brer Rabbit, deyer nice, en fresh, en tender,'
sez Brer Fox, sezee.

" Den Brer Rabbit sorter pull his mustarsh, en say :
' You ain't got no calamus root, is you, Brer Fox ? I
done got so now dat I can't eat no chicken 'ceppin she's

seasoned up wid calamus root.'   En wid dat Brer Rabbit lipt out er de do' and dodge 'mong de bushes, en sot dar watchin' fer Brer Fox; en he ain't watch long, nudder, kaze Brer Fox flung off de flannil en crope out er de house en got whar he could cloze in on Brer Rabbit, en bimeby Brer Rabbit holler out: ' Oh, Brer Fox! I'll des put yo' calamus root out yer on dish yer stump.   Better come git it while hit's fresh,' and wid dat Brer Rabbit gallop off home.   En Brer Fox ain't never kotch 'im yit, en w'at's mo', honey, he ain't gwineter."

II.

THE WONDERFUL TAR-BABY STORY.

" DIDN'T the fox *never* catch the rabbit, Uncle Remus? " asked the little boy the next evening.

" He come mighty nigh it, honey, sho's you born— Brer Fox did.   One day atter Brer Rabbit fool 'im wid dat calamus root, Brer Fox went ter wuk en got 'im some tar, en mix it wid some turkentime, en fix up a contrapshun wat he call a Tar-Baby, en he tuck dish yer Tar-Baby en he sot 'er in de big road, en den he lay off in de bushes fer to see wat de news wuz gwineter be.   En he didn't hatter wait long, nudder, kaze bimeby here come Brer Rabbit pacin' down de road—lippity-clippity, clippity-lippity—dez ez sassy ez a jay-bird. Brer Fox, he lay low.   Brer Rabbit come prancin' 'long

twel he spy de Tar-Baby, en den he fotch up on his behime legs like he wuz 'stonished.   De Tar-Baby, she
sot dar, she did, en Brer Fox, he lay low.

"'Mawnin'!' sez Brer Rabbit, sezee—'nice wedder
dis mawnin',' sezee.

"Tar-Baby ain't sayin' nothin', en Brer Fox, he lay
low.

"'How duz yo' sym'tums seem ter segashuate?' sez
Brer Rabbit, sezee.

"Brer Fox, he wink his eye slow, en lay low, en de
Tar-Baby, she ain't sayin' nothin'.

"'How you come on, den?   Is you deaf?' sez Brer
Rabbit, sezee.   'Kaze if you is, I kin holler louder,'
sezee.

" Tar-Baby stay still, en Brer Fox, he lay low.

" ' Youer stuck up, dat's w'at you is,' says Brer
Rabbit, sezee, ' en
I'm   gwineter
kyore you, dat's
w'at I'm a gwine-
ter do,' sezee.

" Brer Fox, he
sorter chuckle in
his stummuck, he
did, but Tar-Baby
ain't sayin' noth-
in'.

" ' I'm gwine-
ter larn you how-
ter talk ter 'spect-
tubble fokes ef hit's de las' ack,' sez Brer Rabbit,
sezee. ' Ef you don't take off dat hat en tell me
howdy, I'm gwineter bus' you wide open,' sezee.

" Tar-Baby stay still, en Brer Fox, he lay low.

" Brer Rabbit keep on axin' 'im, en de Tar-Baby,
she keep on sayin' nothin', twel present'y Brer Rabbit
draw back wid his fis', he did, en blip he tuck 'er side
er de head. Right dar's whar he broke his merlasses
jug. His fis' stuck, en he can't pull loose. De tar hilt
'im. But Tar-Baby, she stay still, en Brer Fox, he lay
low.

" ' Ef you don't lemme loose, I'll knock you agin,'

sez Brer Rabbit, sezee, en wid dat he fotch 'er a wipe wid de udder han', en dat stuck. Tar-Baby, she ain't sayin' nothin', en Brer Fox, he lay low.

" ' Tu'n me loose, fo' I kick de natal stuffin' outen you,' sez Brer Rabbit, sezee, but de Tar-Baby, she ain't sayin' nothin'. She des hilt on, en den Brer Rabbit

lose de use er his feet in de same way. Brer Fox, he lay low. Den Brer Rabbit squall out dat ef de Tar-Baby don't tu'n 'im loose he butt 'er cranksided. En den he butted, en his head got stuck. Den Brer Fox, he sa'ntered fort', lookin' des ez innercent ez one er yo' mammy's mockin'-birds.

" ' Howdy, Brer Rabbit,' sez Brer Fox, sezee. ' You

look sorter stuck up dis mawnin',' sezee, en den he
rolled on de groun', en laughed en laughed twel he
couldn't laugh no mo'. 'I speck you'll take dinner
wid me dis time, Brer Rabbit. I done laid in some
calamus root, en I ain't gwineter take no skuse,' sez
Brer Fox, sezee."

Here Uncle Remus paused, and drew a two-pound
yam out of the ashes.

"Did the fox eat the rabbit?" asked the little boy
to whom the story had been told.

"Dat's all de fur de tale goes," replied the old man.
"He mout, en den agin he moutent. Some say Jedge
B'ar come 'long en loosed 'im—some say he didn't. I
hear Miss Sally callin'. You better run 'long."

III.

WHY MR. POSSUM LOVES PEACE.

"ONE night," said Uncle Remus—taking Miss Sally's little boy on his knee, and stroking the child's hair
thoughtfully and caressingly—"one night Brer Possum
call by fer Brer Coon, 'cordin' ter greement, en atter
gobblin' up a dish er fried greens en smokin' a seegyar,
dey rambled fort' fer ter see how de ballance er de settlement wuz gittin' 'long. Brer Coon, he wuz one er
deze yer natchul pacers, en he racked 'long same ez

Mars John's bay pony, en Brer Possum he went in a han'-gallup; en dey got over heap er groun', mon. Brer Possum, he got his belly full er 'simmons, en Brer Coon, he scoop up a 'bunnunce er frogs en tadpoles. Dey amble 'long, dey did, des ez sociable ez a basket er kittens, twel bimeby dey hear Mr. Dog talkin' ter hisse'f way off in de woods.

"'Spozen he runs up on us, Brer Possum, w'at you gwineter do?' sez Brer Coon, sezee. Brer Possum sorter laugh 'round de cornders un his mouf.

"'Oh, ef he come, Brer Coon, I'm gwineter stan' by you,' sez Brer Possum. 'W'at you gwineter do?' sezee.

"'Who? me?' sez Brer Coon. 'Ef he run up onter me, I lay I give 'im one twis',' sezee."

"Did the dog come?" asked the little boy.

"Go 'way, honey!" responded the old man, in an impressive tone. "Go way! Mr. Dog, he come en he come a zoonin'. En he ain't wait fer ter say howdy, nudder. He des sail inter de two un um. De ve'y fus pas he make Brer Possum fetch a grin fum year ter year, en keel over like he wuz dead. Den Mr. Dog, he sail inter Brer Coon, en right dar's whar he drap his money purse, kaze Brer Coon wuz cut out fer dat kinder bizness, en he fa'rly wipe up de face er de yeth wid 'im. You better b'leeve dat w'en Mr. Dog got a chance to make hisse'f skase he tuck it, en w'at der wuz lef' un him went skaddlin' thoo de woods like hit

wuz shot outen a muskit. En Brer Coon, he sorter
lick his cloze inter shape en rack off, en Brer Possum,
he lay dar like he
wuz dead, twel
bimeby he raise up

sorter keerful like, en
w'en he fine de coas'
cle'r he scramble up en
scamper off like sumpin was atter 'im."

Here Uncle Remus paused long enough to pick up
a live coal of fire in his fingers, transfer it to the palm
of his hand, and thence to his clay pipe, which he had
been filling—a proceeding that was viewed by the little
boy with undisguised admiration. The old man then
proceeded :

"Nex' time Brer Possum met Brer Coon, Brer Coon 'fuse ter 'spon' ter his howdy, en dis make Brer Possum feel mighty bad, seein' ez how dey useter make so many 'scurshuns tergedder.

"'W'at make you hol' yo' head so high, Brer Coon?' sez Brer Possum, sezee.

"'I ain't runnin' wid cowerds deze days,' sez Brer Coon. 'W'en I wants you I'll sen' fer you,' sezee.

"Den Brer Possum git mighty mad.

"'Who's enny cowerd?' sezee.

"'You is,' sez Brer Coon, 'dat's who. I ain't so-shatin' wid dem w'at lays down on de groun' en plays dead w'en dar's a free fight gwine on,' sezee.

"Den Brer Possum grin en laugh fit to kill hisse'f.

"'Lor', Brer Coon, you don't speck I done dat kaze I wuz 'feared, duz you?' sezee. 'W'y I want no mo' 'feared dan you is dis minnit. W'at wuz dey fer ter be skeered un?' sezee. 'I know'd you'd git away wid Mr. Dog ef I didn't, en I des lay dar watchin' you shake him, waitin' fer ter put in w'en de time come,' sezee.

"Brer Coon tu'n up his nose.

"'Dat's a mighty likely tale,' sezee, 'w'en Mr. Dog ain't mo'n tech you 'fo' you keel over, en lay dar stiff,' sezee.

"'Dat's des w'at I wuz gwineter tell you 'bout,' sez Brer Possum, sezee. 'I want no mo' skeer'd dan you is right now, en' I wuz fixin' fer ter give Mr. Dog a sample er my jaw,' sezee, ' but I'm de most ticklish chap w'at you ever laid eyes on, en no sooner did Mr.

Dog put his nose down yer 'mong my ribs dan I got ter laughin', en I laughed twel I ain't had no use er my lim's,' sezee, ' en it's a mussy unto Mr. Dog dat I wuz ticklish, kaze

a little mo' en I'd e't 'im up,' sezee. ' I don't mine fightin', Brer Coon, no mo' dan you duz,' sezee, ' but I declar' ter grashus ef I kin stan' ticklin'. Git me in a row whar dey ain't no ticklin' 'lowed, en I'm your man,' sezee.

" En down ter dis day "—continued Uncle Remus, watching the smoke from his pipe curl upward over the little boy's head—" down ter dis day, Brer Possum's bound ter s'render w'en you tech him in de short ribs, en he'll laugh ef he knows he's gwineter be smashed fer it."

IV.

HOW MR. RABBIT WAS TOO SHARP FOR MR. FOX.

" UNCLE REMUS," said the little boy one evening, when he had found the old man with little or nothing to do, " did the fox kill and eat the rabbit when he caught him with the Tar-Baby ? "

" Law, honey, ain't I tell you 'bout dat ? " replied the old darkey, chuckling slyly. " I 'clar ter grashus I ought er tole you dat, but old man Nod wuz ridin' cn my eyeleds 'twel a leetle mo'n I'd a dis'member'd my own name, en den on to dat here come yo' mammy hollerin' atter you.

" W'at I tell you w'en I fus' begin ? I tole you Brer Rabbit wuz a monstus soon creetur; leas'ways dat's w'at I laid out fer ter tell you. Well, den, honey, don't you go en make no udder calkalashuns, kaze in dem days Brer Rabbit en his fambly wuz at de head er de gang w'en enny racket wuz on han', en dar dey stayed. 'Fo' you begins fer ter wipe yo' eyes 'bout Brer Rabbit, you wait en see whar'bouts Brer Rabbit gwineter fetch up at. But dat's needer yer ner dar.

" W'en Brer Fox fine Brer Rabbit mixt up wid de Tar-Baby, he feel mighty good, en he roll on de groun' en laff. Bimeby he up'n say, sezee :

" ' Well, I speck I got you dis time, Brer Rabbit, sezee ; ' maybe I ain't, but I speck I is. You been run-

nin' roun' here sassin' atter me a mighty long time, but
I speck you done come ter de een' er de row. You bin
cuttin' up yo' capers en bouncin' 'roun' in dis neighber-
hood ontwel you come ter b'leeve yo'se'f de boss er de
whole gang. En den youer allers some'rs whar you got

no bizness,' sez Brer Fox, sezee. 'Who ax you fer ter
come en strike up a 'quaintance wid dish yer Tar-Baby?
En who stuck you up dar whar you iz? Nobody in de
roun' worril. You des tuck en jam yo'se'f on dat Tar-
Baby widout waitin' fer enny invite,' sez Brer Fox,
sezee, 'en dar you is, en dar you'll stay twel I fixes up
a bresh-pile and fires her up, kaze I'm gwineter bobby-
cue you dis day, sho,' sez Brer Fox, sezee.

"Den Brer Rabbit talk mighty 'umble.

" ' I don't keer w'at you do wid me, Brer Fox,'
sezee, ' so you don't fling me in dat brier-patch. Roas'
me, Brer Fox,' sezee, ' but don't fling me in dat brier-
patch,' sezee.

" ' Hit's so much trouble fer ter kindle a fier,' sez
Brer Fox, sezee, ' dat I speck I'll hatter hang you,'
sezee.

" ' Hang me des ez high as you please, Brer Fox,'
sez Brer Rabbit, sezee, ' but do fer de Lord's sake don't
fling me in dat brier-patch,' sezee.

" ' I ain't got no string,' sez Brer Fox, sezee, ' en
now I speck I'll hatter drown you,' sezee.

" ' Drown me des ez deep ez you please, Brer Fox,'
sez Brer Rabbit, sezee, ' but do don't fling me in dat
brier-patch,' sezee.

" ' Dey ain't no water nigh,' sez Brer Fox, sezee,
' en now I speck I'll hatter skin you,' sezee.

" ' Skin me, Brer Fox,' sez Brer Rabbit, sezee,
' snatch out my eyeballs, t'ar out my years by de roots,
en cut off my legs,' sezee, ' but do please, Brer Fox,
don't fling me in dat brier-patch,' sezee.

" Co'se Brer Fox wanter hurt Brer Rabbit bad ez
he kin, so he cotch 'im by de behime legs en slung 'im
right in de middle er de brier-patch. Dar wuz a con-
siderbul flutter whar Brer Rabbit struck de bushes, en
Brer Fox sorter hang 'roun' fer ter see w'at wuz gwineter happen. Bimeby he hear somebody call 'im, en way
up de hill he see Brer Rabbit settin' cross-legged on a

chinkapin log koamin' de pitch outen his har wid a chip. Den Brer Fox know dat he bin swop off mighty

bad. Brer Rabbit wuz bleedzed fer ter fling back some er his sass, en he holler out:

"'Bred en bawn in a brier-patch, Brer Fox—bred en bawn in a brier-patch!' en wid dat he skip out des ez lively ez a cricket in de embers."

V.

THE STORY OF THE DELUGE AND HOW IT CAME ABOUT.

"ONE time," said Uncle Remus—adjusting his spectacles so as to be able to see how to thread a large darning-needle with which he was patching his coat—"one time, way back yander, 'fo' you wuz borned, honey, en 'fo' Mars John er Miss Sally wuz borned—way back yander 'fo' enny un us wuz borned, de anemils en de creeturs sorter 'lecshuneer roun' 'mong deyselves, twel at las' dey 'greed fer ter have a 'sembly. In dem days," continued the old man, observing a look of incredulity

on the little boy's face, "in dem days creeturs had lots mo' sense dan dey got now; let 'lone dat, dey had sense

same like folks.   Hit was tech en go wid um, too, mon,
en w'en dey make up der mines w'at hatter be done,
'twant mo'n menshun'd 'fo' hit wuz done.   Well, dey
'lected dat dey hatter hole er · 'sembly fer ter sorter
straighten out marters en hear de complaints, en w'en
de day come dey wuz on han'.   De Lion, he wuz dar,
kase he wuz de king, en he hatter be dar.   De Rhynos-
syhoss, he wuz dar, en de Elephent, he wuz dar, en de
Cammils, en de Cows, en plum down ter de Crawfishes,
dey wuz dar.   Dey wuz all dar.   En w'en de Lion
shuck his mane, en tuck his seat in de big cheer, den
de sesshun begun fer ter commence."

"What did they do, Uncle Remus?" asked the little
boy.

"I can't skacely call to mine 'zackly w'at dey did
do, but dey spoke speeches, en hollered, en cusst, en
flung der langwidge 'roun' des like w'en yo' daddy wuz
gwineter run fer de legislater en got lef'.   Howsomever,
dey 'ranged der 'fairs, en splained der bizness.   Bimeby,
w'ile dey wuz 'sputin' 'longer one er nudder, de Elephent trompled on one er de Crawfishes.   Co'se w'en
dat creetur put his foot down, w'atsumever's under dar
wuz boun' fer ter be squshed, en dey wa'n't nuff er dat
Crawfish lef' fer ter tell dat he'd bin dar.

"Dis make de udder Crawfishes mighty mad, en
dey sorter swarmed tergedder en draw'd up a kinder
peramble wid some wharfo'es in it, en read her out in
de 'sembly.   But, bless grashus! sech a racket wuz a

gwine on dat nobody ain't hear it, 'ceppin may be de
Mud Turkle en de Spring Lizzud, en dere enfloons wuz
pow'ful lackin'.

"Bimeby, w'iles de Nunicorn wuz 'sputin' wid de
Lion, en w'ile de Hyener wuz a laughin' ter hisse'f, de
Elephent squshed anudder one er de Crawfishes, en a
little mo'n he'd er ruint de Mud Turkle. Den de Crawfishes, w'at dey wuz lef' un um, swarmed tergedder en
draw'd up anudder peramble wid sum mo' wharfo'es;
but dey might ez well er sung Ole Dan Tucker ter a
harrycane. De udder creeturs wuz too busy wid der
fussin' fer ter 'spon' unto de Crawfishes. So dar dey
wuz, de Crawfishes, en dey didn't know w'at minnit
wuz gwineter be de nex'; en dey kep' on gittin madder
en madder en skeerder en skeerder, twel bimeby dey
gun de wink ter de Mud Turkle en de Spring Lizzud,
en den dey bo'd little holes in de groun' en went down
outer sight."

"Who did, Uncle Remus?" asked the little
boy.

"De Crawfishes, honey. Dey bo'd inter de groun'
en kep' on bo'in twel dey onloost de fountains er de
earf; en de waters squirt out, en riz higher en higher
twel de hills wuz kivvered, en de creeturs wuz all
drownded; en all bekaze dey let on 'mong deyselves
dat dey wuz bigger dan de Crawfishes."

Then the old man blew the ashes from a smoking
yam, and proceeded to remove the peeling.

"Where was the ark, Uncle Remus?" the little boy inquired, presently.

"W'ich ark's dat?" asked the old man, in a tone of well-feigned curiosity.

"Noah's ark," replied the child.

"Don't you pester wid ole man Noah, honey. I boun' he tuck keer er dat ark. Dat's w'at he wuz dar fer, en dat's w'at he done. Leas'ways, dat's w'at dey tells me. But don't you bodder longer dat ark, 'ceppin' your mammy fetches it up. Dey mout er bin two deloojes, en den agin dey moutent. Ef dey wuz enny ark in dish yer w'at de Crawfishes brung on, I ain't heern tell un it, en w'en dey ain't no arks 'roun', I ain't got no time fer ter make um en put um in dar. Hit's gittin' yo' bedtime, honey."

MR. RABBIT GROSSLY DECEIVES MR. FOX.

ONE evening when the little boy, whose nights with Uncle Remus were as entertaining as those Arabian ones of blessed memory, had finished supper and hurried out to sit with his venerable patron, he found the old man in great glee. Indeed, Uncle Remus was talking and laughing to himself at such a rate that the little boy was afraid he had company. The truth is, Uncle Remus had heard the child coming, and, when the rosy-cheeked chap put his head in at the door, was engaged in a monologue, the burden of which seemed to be—

> "Ole Molly Har',
> W'at you doin' dar,
> Settin' in de cornder
> Smokin' yo' seegyar?"

As a matter of course this vague allusion reminded the little boy of the fact that the wicked Fox was still in pursuit of the Rabbit, and he immediately put his curiosity in the shape of a question.

"Uncle Remus, did the Rabbit have to go clean away when he got loose from the Tar-Baby?"

"Bless gracious, honey, dat he didn't. Who? Him? You dunno nuthin' 'tall 'bout Brer Rabbit ef dat's de way you puttin' 'im down. W'at he gwine 'way fer? He moughter stayed sorter close twel de

piten rub off'n his ha'r, but twern't menny days 'fo' he
wuz lopin' up en down de neighborhood same ez ever,
en I dunno ef he wern't mo' sassier dan befo'.

"Seem like dat de tale 'bout how he got mixt
up wid de Tar-Baby got 'roun' 'mongst de nabers.
Leas'ways, Miss Meadows en de gals got win' un' it, en
de nex' time Brer Rabbit paid um a visit Miss Meadows
tackled 'im 'bout it, en de gals sot up a monstus giggle-
ment. Brer Rabbit, he sot up des ez cool ez a cow-
cumber, he did, en let 'em run on."

"Who was Miss Meadows, Uncle Remus?" inquired the little boy.

"Don't ax me, honey. She wuz in de tale, Miss
Meadows en de gals wuz, en de tale I give you like hi't
wer' gun ter me. Brer Rabbit, he sot dar, he did,
sorter lam' like, en den bimeby he cross his legs, he
did, and wink his eye slow, en up and say, sezee:

"'Ladies, Brer Fox wuz my daddy's ridin'-hoss fer
thirty year; maybe mo', but thirty year dat I knows
un,' sezee; en den he paid um his 'specks, en tip his
beaver, en march off, he did, des ez stiff en ez stuck up
ez a fire-stick.

"Nex' day, Brer Fox cum a callin', and w'en he
gun fer ter laugh 'bout Brer Rabbit, Miss Meadows en
de gals, dey ups en tells 'im 'bout w'at Brer Rabbit say.
Den Brer Fox grit his tushes sho' nuff, he did, en he
look mighty dumpy, but w'en he riz fer ter go he up
en say, sezee:

"'Ladies, I ain't 'sputin' w'at you say, but I'll make Brer Rabbit chaw up his words en spit um out right yer whar you kin see 'im,' sezee, en wid dat off Brer Fox put.

"En w'en he got in de big road, he shuck de dew off'n his tail, en made a straight shoot fer Brer Rabbit's house. W'en he got dar, Brer Rabbit wuz spectin' un 'im, en de do' wuz shet fas'. Brer Fox knock. Nobody ain't ans'er. Brer Fox knock. Nobody ans'er. Den he knock agin—blam! blam! Den Brer Rabbit holler out mighty weak:

"'Is dat you, Brer Fox? I want you ter run en fetch de doctor. Dat bait er pusly w'at I e't dis mawnin' is gittin' 'way wid me. Do, please, Brer Fox, run quick,' sez Brer Rabbit, sezee.

"'I come atter you, Brer Rabbit,' sez Brer Fox,

sezee. ' Dar's gwineter be a party up at Miss Meadows's,' sezee. ' All de gals 'll be dere, en I promus' dat
I'd fetch you. De gals, dey 'lowed dat hit wouldn't be
no party 'ceppin' I fotch you,' sez Brer Fox, sezee.

" Den Brer Rabbit say he wuz too sick, en Brer
Fox say he wuzzent, en dar dey had it up and down,
'sputin' en contendin'. Brer Rabbit say he can't walk.
Brer Fox say he tote 'im. Brer Rabbit say how?
Brer Fox say in his arms. Brer Rabbit say he drap
'im. Brer Fox 'low he won't. Bimeby Brer Rabbit
say he go ef Brer Fox tote 'im on his back. Brer Fox
say he would. Brer Rabbit say he can't ride widout a
saddle. Brer Fox say he git de saddle. Brer Rabbit
say he can't set in saddle less he have bridle fer ter hol'
by. Brer Fox say he git de bridle. Brer Rabbit say
he can't ride widout bline bridle, kaze Brer Fox be
shyin' at stumps 'long de road, en fling 'im off. Brer
Fox say he git bline bridle. Den Brer Rabbit say he
go. Den Brer Fox say he ride Brer Rabbit mos' up
ter Miss Meadows's, en den he could git down en walk
de balance er de way. Brer Rabbit 'greed, en den
Brer Fox lipt out atter de saddle en de bridle.

" Co'se Brer Rabbit know de game dat Brer Fox
wuz fixin' fer ter play, en he 'termin' fer ter outdo 'im,
en by de time he koam his ha'r en twis' his mustarsh,
en sorter rig up, yer come Brer Fox, saddle en bridle
on, en lookin' ez peart ez a circus pony. He trot up
ter de do' en stan' dar pawin' de ground en chompin'

de bit same like sho 'nuff hoss, en Brer Rabbit he mount, he did, en dey amble off. Brer Fox can't see behime wid de bline bridle on, but bimeby he feel Brer Rabbit raise one er his foots.

" ' W'at you doin' now, Brer Rabbit?' sezee.

" 'Short'nin' de lef stir'p, Brer Fox,' sezee.

" Bimeby Brer Rabbit raise up de udder foot.

" ' W'at you doin' now, Brer Rabbit?' sezee.

" ' Pullin' down my pants, Brer Fox,' sezee.

" All de time, bless grashus, honey, Brer Rabbit wer puttin' on his spurrers, en w'en dey got close to Miss Meadows's, whar Brer Rabbit wuz to git off, en

Brer Fox made a motion fer ter stan' still, Brer Rabbit slap de spurrers inter Brer Fox flanks, en you better b'leeve he got over groun'. W'en dey got ter de house, Miss Meadows en all de gals wuz settin' on de peazzer, en stidder stoppin' at de gate, Brer Rabbit rid on by, he did, en den come gallopin' down de road en up ter de hoss-rack, w'ich he hitch Brer Fox at, en den he santer inter de house, he did, en shake han's wid de gals, en set dar, smokin' his seegyar same ez a town man. Bimeby he draw in a long puff, en den let hit out in a cloud, en squar hisse'f back en holler out, he did:

" 'Ladies, ain't I done tell you Brer Fox wuz de ridin'-hoss fer our fambly? He sorter losin' his gait now, but I speck I kin fetch 'im all right in a mont' er so,' sezee.

" En den Brer Rabbit sorter grin, he did, en de gals giggle, en Miss Meadows, she praise up de pony, en dar wuz Brer Fox hitch fas' ter de rack, en couldn't he'p hisse'f."

" Is that all, Uncle Remus?" asked the little boy as the old man paused.

"Dat ain't all, honey, but 'twon't do fer ter give out too much cloff fer ter cut one pa'r pants," replied the old man sententiously.

VII.

MR. FOX IS AGAIN VICTIMIZED.

WHEN "Miss Sally's" little boy went to Uncle Remus the next night to hear the conclusion of the adventure in which the Rabbit made a riding-horse of the Fox to the great enjoyment and gratification of Miss Meadows and the girls, he found the old man in a bad humor.

"I ain't tellin' no tales ter bad chilluns," said Uncle Remus curtly.

"But, Uncle Remus, I ain't bad," said the little boy plaintively.

"Who dat chunkin' dem chickens dis mawnin'? Who dat knockin' out fokes's eyes wid dat Yallerbammer sling des 'fo' dinner? Who dat sickin' dat pinter puppy atter my pig? Who dat scatterin' my ingun sets? Who dat flingin' rocks on top er my house, w'ich a little mo' en one un em would er drap spang on my head?"

"Well, now, Uncle Remus, I didn't go to do it. I won't do so any more. Please, Uncle Remus, if you will tell me, I'll run to the house and bring you some tea-cakes."

"Seein' um's better'n hearin' tell un um," replied the old man, the severity of his countenance relaxing somewhat; but the little boy darted out, and in a few minutes came running back with his pockets full and his hands full.

"I lay yo' mammy 'll 'spishun dat de rats' stummucks is widenin' in dis neighborhood w'en she come fer ter count up 'er cakes," said Uncle Remus, with a chuckle. "Deze," he continued, dividing the cakes into two equal parts—"dese I'll tackle now, en dese I'll lay by fer Sunday.

"Lemme see. I mos' dis'member wharbouts Brer Fox en Brer Rabbit wuz."

"The rabbit rode the fox to Miss Meadows's, and hitched him to the horse-rack," said the little boy.

"W'y co'se he did," said Uncle Remus. "Co'se he did. Well, Brer Rabbit rid Brer Fox up, he did, en tied 'im to de rack, en den sot out in de peazzer wid de gals a smokin' er his seegyar wid mo' proudness dan w'at you mos' ever see. Dey talk, en dey sing, en dey play on de peanner, de gals did, twel bimeby hit  come time fer Brer Rabbit fer to be gwine, en he tell um all good-by, en strut out to de hoss-rack same's ef he wuz de king er de patter-rollers,* en den he mount Brer Fox en ride off.

"Brer Fox ain't sayin' nuthin' 'tall. He des rack off, he did, en keep his mouf shet, en Brer Rabbit know'd der wuz bizness cookin' up fer him, en he feel monstus skittish. Brer Fox amble on twel he git in de long lane, outer sight er Miss Meadows's house, en den he tu'n loose, he did. He rip en he r'ar, en he cuss, en he swar ; he snort en he cavort."

"What was he doing that for, Uncle Remus ?" the little boy inquired.

" He wuz tryin' fer ter fling Brer Rabbit off'n his back, bless yo' soul ! But he des might ez well er rastle wid his own shadder. Every time he hump hisse'f Brer Rabbit slap de spurrers in 'im, en dar dey had it, up en down. Brer Fox fa'rly to' up de groun' he did, en he jump so high en he jump so quick dat he mighty nigh snatch his own tail off. Dey kep' on gwine on dis way twel bimeby Brer Fox lay down en roll over, he did, en dis sorter onsettle Brer Rabbit, but by de time Brer Fox got back on his footses agin, Brer Rabbit wuz gwine thoo de under-bresh mo' samer dan a race-hoss. Brer Fox he lit out

---

* Patrols. In the country districts, order was kept on the plantations at night by the knowledge that they were liable to be visited at any moment by the patrols. Hence a song current among the negroes, the chorus of which was :

"Run, nigger, run ; patter-roller ketch you—
Run, nigger, run ; hit's almos' day."

atter 'im, he did, en he push Brer Rabbit so close
dat it wuz 'bout all 'he could do fer ter git in a
holler tree. Hole too little fer Brer Fox fer
ter git in, en he hatter lay down
en res' en gedder his mine tergedder.

"While he wuz layin' dar,
Mr. Buzzard come floppin'
'long, en seein' Brer Fox
stretch out on de groun',
he lit en view de pre-
musses. Den Mr. Buz-
zard sorter shake his wing,
en put his head on one side,
en say to hisse'f like, sezee:

"'Brer Fox dead, en I so sorry,' sezee.

"'No I ain't dead, nudder,'
sez Brer Fox, sezee. 'I
got ole man
Rabbit pent
up in yer,'
sezee, 'en
I'm a gwine-

ter git 'im dis time ef it take twel Chris'mus,' sezee.

"Den, atter some mo' palaver, Brer Fox make a bargain dat Mr. Buzzard wuz ter watch de hole, en keep Brer Rabbit dar wiles Brer Fox went atter his axe. Den Brer Fox, he lope off, he did, en Mr. Buzzard, he tuck up his stan' at de hole. Bimeby, w'en all git still, Brer Rabbit sorter scramble down close ter de hole, he did, en holler out:

"'Brer Fox! Oh! Brer Fox!'

"Brer Fox done gone, en nobody say nuthin'. Den Brer Rabbit squall out like he wuz mad; sezee:

"'You needn't talk less you wanter,' sezee; 'I knows youer dar, en I ain't keerin',' sezee. 'I des wanter tell you dat I wish mighty bad Brer Tukkey Buzzard wuz here,' sezee.

"Den Mr. Buzzard try ter talk like Brer Fox:

"'W'at you want wid Mr. Buzzard?' sezee.

"'Oh, nuthin' in 'tickler, 'cep' dere's de fattes' gray squir'l in yer dat ever I see,' sezee, 'en ef Brer Tukkey Buzzard wuz 'roun' he'd be mighty glad fer ter git 'im,' sezee.

"'How Mr. Buzzard gwine ter git 'im?' sez de Buzzard, sezee.

"'Well, dar's a little hole roun' on de udder side er de tree,' sez Brer Rabbit, sezee, 'en ef Brer Tukkey Buzzard wuz here so he could take up his stan' dar,' sezee, 'I'd drive dat squir'l out,' sezee.

"'Drive 'im out, den,' sez Mr. Buzzard, sezee, 'en I'll see dat Brer Tukkey Buzzard gits 'im,' sezee.

"Den Brer Rabbit kick up a racket, like he wer' drivin' sumpin' out, en Mr. Buzzard he rush 'roun' fer ter ketch de squir'l, en Brer Rabbit, he dash out, he did, en he des fly fer home."

At this point Uncle Remus took one of the tea-cakes, held

his head back, opened his mouth, dropped the cake in with a sudden motion, looked at the little boy with an expression of astonishment, and then closed his eyes, and begun to chew, mumbling as an accompaniment the plaintive tune of "Don't you Grieve atter Me."

The *séance* was over; but, before the little boy went into the "big house," Uncle Remus laid his rough hand tenderly on the child's shoulder, and re-marked, in a confidential tone:

"Honey, you mus' git up soon Chris'mus mawnin' en open de do'; kase I'm gwineter bounce in on Marse John en Miss Sally, en holler Chris'mus gif' des like I useter endurin' de farmin' days fo' de war, w'en ole Miss wuz 'live. I boun' dey don't fergit de ole nigger, nudder. W'en you hear me callin' de pigs, honey, you des hop up en onfassen de do'. I lay I'll give Marse John one er dese yer 'sprize parties."

VIII.

MR. FOX IS "OUTDONE" BY MR. BUZZARD.

"Ef I don't run inter no mistakes," remarked Uncle Remus, as the little boy came tripping in to see him after supper, "Mr. Tukkey Buzzard wuz gyardin' de holler whar Brer Rabbit went in at, en w'ich he come out un."

The silence of the little boy verified the old man's recollection.

"Well, Mr. Buzzard, he feel mighty lonesome, he did, but he done prommust Brer Fox dat he'd stay, en he 'termin' fer ter sorter hang 'roun' en jine in de joke. En he ain't hatter wait long, nudder, kase bimeby yer come Brer Fox gallopin' thoo de woods wid his axe on his shoulder.

"'How you speck Brer Rabbit gittin' on, Brer Buzzard?' sez Brer Fox, sezee.

"'Oh, he in dar,' sez Brer Buzzard, sezee. 'He mighty still, dough. I speck he takin' a nap,' sezee.

"'Den I'm des in time fer ter wake 'im up,' sez Brer Fox, sezee. En wid dat he fling off his coat, en spit in his han's, en grab de axe. Den he draw back en come down on de tree—pow! En eve'y time he come down wid de axe—pow!—Mr. Buzzard, he step high, he did, en holler out:

"'Oh, he in dar, Brer Fox. He in dar, sho.'

"En eve'y time a chip ud fly off, Mr. Buzzard, he'd jump, en dodge, en hole his head sideways, he would, en holler:

"'He in dar, Brer Fox. I done heerd 'im. He in dar, sho.'

"En Brer Fox, he lammed away at dat holler tree, he did, like a man maulin' rails, twel bimeby, atter he done got de tree mos' cut thoo, he stop fer ter ketch his bref, en he seed Mr. Buzzard laughin' behime his back, he did, en right den en dar, widout gwine enny fudder, Brer Fox, he smelt a rat. But Mr. Buzzard, he keep on holler'n :

"'He in dar, Brer Fox. He in dar, sho. I done seed 'im.'

"Den Brer Fox, he make like he peepin' up de holler, en he say, sezee :

"'Run yer, Brer Buzzard, en look ef dis ain't Brer Rabbit's foot hanging down yer.'

"En Mr. Buzzard, he come steppin' up, he did, same ez ef he wer treddin' on kurkle-burs, en he stick his head in de hole ; en no sooner did he done dat dan Brer Fox grab 'im. Mr. Buzzard flap his wings, en scramble 'roun' right smartually, he did, but 'twant no use. Brer Fox had de 'vantage er de grip, he did, en he hilt 'im right down ter de groun'. Den Mr. Buzzard squall out, sezee :

"'Lemme 'lone, Brer Fox. Tu'n me loose,' sezee ; 'Brer Rabbit'll git out. Youer gittin' close at 'im,' sezee, 'en leb'm mo' licks'll fetch 'im,' sezee.

"'I'm nigher ter you, Brer Buzzard,' sez Brer Fox,

sezee, 'dan I'll be ter Brer Rabbit dis day,' sezee.
'W'at you fool me fer?' sezee.

"'Lemme 'lone, Brer Fox,' sez Mr. Buzzard, sezee;
'my ole 'oman waitin' fer me. Brer Rabbit in dar,'
sezee.

"'Dar's a bunch er his fur on dat black-be'y bush,'
sez Brer Fox, sezee, 'en dat ain't de way he come,'
sezee.

"Den Mr. Buzzard up'n tell Brer Fox how 'twuz,
en he low'd, Mr. Buzzard did, dat Brer Rabbit wuz de
lowdownest w'atsizname w'at he ever run up wid.
Den Brer Fox say, sezee:

"'Dat's needer here ner dar, Brer Buzzard,' sezee.
'I lef' you yer fer ter watch dish yere 'iole, en I lef'
Brer Rabbit in dar. I comes back en I fines you at de
hole en Brer Rabbit ain't in dar,' sezee. 'I'm gwineter make you pay fer't. I done bin tampered wid twel
plum' down ter de sap sucker'll set on a log en sassy
me. I'm gwinter fling you in a bresh-heap en burn
you up,' sezee.

"'Ef you fling me on der fier, Brer Fox, I'll fly
'way,' sez Mr. Buzzard, sezee.

"'Well, den, I'll settle yo' hash right now,' sez
Brer Fox, sezee, en wid dat he grab Mr. Buzzard by de
tail, he did, en make fer ter dash 'im 'gin de groun',
but des 'bout dat time de tail fedders come out, en Mr.
Buzzard sail off like one er dese yer berloons; en ez
he riz, he holler back:

" ' You gimme good start, Brer Fox,' sezee, en Brer Fox sot dar en watch 'im fly outer sight."

" But what be-came of the Rab-bit, Uncle Remus ? " asked the little boy.

" Don't you pes-ter 'longer Brer Rabbit, honey, en don't you fret 'bout 'im.   You'll year whar he went en how he come out.   Dish yer cole snap rastles wid my bones, now," continued the old man, putting on his hat and pick-ing up his walking-stick.   " Hit rastles wid me mons-tus, en I gotter rack 'roun' en see if I kin run up agin some Chris'mus leavin's."

IX.

MISS COW FALLS A VICTIM TO MR. RABBIT.

" UNCLE REMUS," said the little boy, " what became of the Rabbit after he fooled the Buzzard, and got out of the hollow tree ? "

"Who? Brer Rabbit? Bless yo' soul, honey, Brer Rabbit went skippin' 'long home, he did, des ez sassy ez a jay-bird at a sparrer's nes'. He went gallopin' 'long, he did, but he feel mighty tired out, en stiff in his jints, en he wuz mighty nigh dead for sumpin fer ter drink, en bimeby, w'en he got mos' home, he spied ole Miss Cow feedin' roun' in a fiel', he did, en he 'termin' fer ter try his han' wid 'er. Brer Rabbit know mighty well dat Miss Cow won't give 'im no milk, kaze she done 'fuse 'im mo'n once, en w'en his ole 'oman wuz sick, at dat. But never mind dat. Brer Rabbit sorter dance up 'long side er de fence, he did, en holler out:

"'Howdy, Sis Cow,' sez Brer Rabbit, sezee.

"'W'y, howdy, Brer Rabbit,' sez Miss Cow, sez she.

"'How you fine yo'se'f deze days, Sis Cow?' sez Brer Rabbit, sezee.

"'I'm sorter toler'ble, Brer Rabbit; how you come on?' sez Miss Cow, sez she.

"'Oh, I'm des toler'ble myse'f, Sis Cow; sorter linger'n' twix' a bauk en a break-down,' sez Brer Rabbit, sezee.

"'How yo' fokes, Brer Rabbit?' sez Miss Cow, sez she.

"'Dey er des middlin', Sis Cow; how Brer Bull gittin' on?' sez Brer Rabbit, sezee.

"'Sorter so-so,' sez Miss Cow, sez she.

"'Dey er some mighty

nice 'simmons up dis tree, Sis Cow,' sez Brer Rabbit, sezee, 'en I'd like mighty well fer ter have some un um,' sezee.

"'How you gwineter git um, Brer Rabbit?' sez she.

"'I 'low'd maybe dat I might ax you fer ter butt 'gin de tree, en shake some down, Sis Cow,' sez Brer Rabbit, sezee.

"C'ose Miss Cow don't wanter diskommerdate Brer Rabbit, en she march up ter de 'simmon tree, she did, en hit it a rap wid'er horns—blam! Now, den," continued Uncle Remus, tearing off the corner of a plug of tobacco and cramming it into his mouth— "now, den, dem 'simmons wuz green ez grass, en na'er one never drap. Den Miss Cow butt de tree —blim! Na'er 'simmon drap. Den Miss Cow sorter back off little, en run agin de tree—blip! No 'simmons never drap. Den Miss Cow back off little fudder, she did, en hi'st her tail on 'er back, en come agin de tree, kerblam! en she come so fas', en she come so hard, twel one 'er her horns went spang thoo de tree, en dar she wuz. She can't go forreds, en she can't go backerds. Dis zackly w'at Brer Rabbit waitin' fer, en he no sooner seed ole Miss Cow all fas'en'd up dan he jump up, he did, en cut de pidjin· wing.

"'Come he'p me out, Brer Rabbit,' sez Miss Cow, sez she.

"'I can't clime, Sis Cow,' sez Brer Rabbit, sezee, 'but I'll run'n tell Brer Bull,' sezee; en wid dat Brer Rabbit put out fer home, en 'twan't long 'fo here he come wid his ole 'oman en all his chilluns, en de las' one er de fambly wuz totin' a pail. De big uns had big pails, en de little uns had little pails. En dey all s'roundid ole Miss Cow, dey did, en you hear me, honey, dey milk't 'er dry. De ole uns milk't en de young

uns milk't, en den w'en dey done got nuff, Brer Rabbit, he up'n say, sezee:

"'I wish you mighty well, Sis
Cow. I 'low'd bein's how dat
you'd hatter sorter camp out all
night dat I'd better
come en swaje yo'
bag,' sezee."

"Do which, Uncle
Remus?" asked the lit-
tle boy.

"Go 'long, honey!
Swaje 'er bag. W'en
cows don't git milk't,
der bag swells, en
youk'n hear um a
moanin' en a beller'n
des like dey wuz gittin'
hurtid.   Dat's w'at
Brer Rabbit done. He
'sembled his fambly,
he did, en he swaje ole
Miss Cow's bag.

"Miss Cow, she stood dar, she did, en she study en
study, en strive fer ter break loose, but de horn done

bin jam in de tree so tight dat twuz way 'fo day in de mornin' 'fo' she loose it. Anyhow hit wuz endurin' er de night, en atter she git loose she sorter graze 'roun', she did, fer ter jestify 'er stummuck. She 'low'd, ole Miss Cow did, dat Brer Rabbit be hoppin' 'long dat way fer ter see how she gittin' on, en she tuck'n lay er trap fer 'im ; en des 'bout sunrise wat'd ole Miss Cow do but march up ter de 'simmon tree en stick er horn back in de hole ? But, bless yo' soul, honey, w'ile she wuz croppin' de grass, she tuck one moufull too menny, kaze w'en she hitch on ter de 'simmon tree agin, Brer Rabbit wuz settin' in de fence cornder a watchin' un 'er. Den Brer Rabbit he say ter hisse'f :

" ' Heyo,' sezee, ' w'at dis yer gwine on now ? Hole yo' hosses, Sis Cow, twel you hear me comin',' sezee.

" En den he crope off down de fence, Brer Rabbit did, en bimeby here he come—lippity-clippity, clippity-lippity—des a sailin' down de big road.

" ' Mornin', Sis Cow,' sez Brer Rabbit, sezee, ' how you come on dis mornin' ? ' sezee.

" ' Po'ly, Brer Rabbit, po'ly,' sez Miss Cow, sez she. ' I ain't had no res' all night,' sez she. ' I can't pull loose,' sez she, ' but ef you'll come en ketch holt er my tail, Brer Rabbit,' sez she, ' I reckin may be I kin fetch my horn out,' sez she. Den Brer Rabbit, he come up little closer, but he ain't gittin' too close.

" ' I speck I'm nigh nuff, Sis Cow,' sez Brer Rabbit, sezee. ' I'm a mighty puny man, en I might git

trompled,' sezee. 'You do de pullin', Sis Cow,' sezee,
'en I'll do de gruntin',' sezee.

"Den Miss Cow, she pull out 'er horn, she did, en
tuck atter Brer Rabbit, en down de big road dey had
it, Brer Rabbit wid his years laid back, en Miss Cow

wid 'er head down en 'er tail curl. Brer Rabbit kep'
on gainin', en bimeby he dart in a brier-patch, en by
de time Miss Cow come 'long he had his head stickin'
out, en his eyes look big ez Miss Sally's chany sassers.

" 'Heyo, Sis Cow! Whar you gwine?' sez Brer
Rabbit, sezee.

" 'Howdy, Brer Big-Eyes,' sez Miss Cow, sez she.
'Is you seed Brer Rabbit go by?'

" 'He des dis minit pass,' sez Brer Rabbit, sezee,
'en he look mighty sick,' sezee.

"En wid dat, Miss Cow tuck down de road like de
dogs wuz atter 'er, en Brer Rabbit, he des lay down dar
in de brier-patch en roll en laugh twel his sides hurtid
'im. He bleedzd ter laff. Fox atter 'im, Buzzard atter
'im, en Cow atter 'im, en dey ain't kotch 'im yit."

X.

MR. TERRAPIN APPEARS UPON THE SCENE.

"Miss Sally's" little boy again occupying the anxious position of auditor, Uncle Remus took the shovel and "put de noses er de chunks tergedder," as he expressed it, and then began:

"One day, atter Sis Cow done run pas' 'er own shadder tryin' fer ter ketch 'im, Brer Rabbit tuck'n

'low dat he wuz gwineter drap in en see Miss Meadows en de gals, en he got out his piece er lookin'-glass en

primp up, he did, en sot out. Gwine canterin' 'long
de road, who should Brer Rabbit run up wid but oie
Brer Tarrypin—de same ole one-en-sixpunce. Brer
Rabbit stop, he did, en rap on de roof er Brer Tarrypin house."

"On the roof of his house, Uncle Remus?" interrupted the little boy.

"Co'se honey, Brer Tarrypin kare his house wid
'im. Rain er shine, hot er cole, strike up wid ole Brer
Tarrypin w'en you will en w'ilst you may, en whar you
fine 'im, dar you'll fine his shanty. Hit's des like I tell
you. So den! Brer Rabbit he rap on de roof er Brer
Tarrypin's house, he did, en ax wuz he in, en Brer
Tarrypin 'low dat he wuz, en den Brer Rabbit, he ax
'im howdy, en den Brer Tarrypin he likewise 'spon'
howdy, en den Brer Rabbit he say whar wuz Brer
Tarrypin gwine, en Brer Tarrypin, he say w'ich he
wern't gwine nowhar skasely. Den Brer Rabbit 'low
he wuz on his way fer ter see Miss Meadows en de
gals, en he ax Brer Tarrypin ef he won't jine in en go
long, en Brer Tarrypin 'spon' he don't keer ef he do,
en den dey sot out. Dey had plenty er time fer con-
fabbin' 'long de way, but bimeby dey got dar, en Miss
Meadows en de gals dey come ter de do', dey did, en
ax um in, en in dey went.

"W'en dey got in, Brer Tarrypin wuz so flat-footed
dat he wuz too low on de flo', en he wern't high nuff
in a cheer, but while dey wuz all scramblin' 'roun'

tryin' fer ter git Brer Tarrypin a cheer, Brer Rabbit, he pick 'im up en put 'im on de shelf whar de water-bucket sot, en ole Brer Tarrypin, he lay back up dar, he did, des es proud ez a nigger wid a cook 'possum.

"Co'se de talk fell on Brer Fox, en Miss Meadows en de gals make a great 'miration 'bout w'at a gaily ridin'-hoss Brer Fox wuz, en dey make lots er fun, en laugh en giggle same like gals duz deze days. Brer Rabbit, he sot dar in de cheer smokin' his seegyar, en he sorter kler up his th'oat, en say, sezee:

"'I'd er rid 'im over dis mawnin', ladies,' sezee, 'but I rid 'im so hard yistiddy dat he went lame in de off fo' leg, en I speck I'll hatter swop 'im off yit,' sezee.

"Den Brer Tarrypin, he up'n say, sezee:

"'Well, ef you gwineter sell 'im, Brer Rabbit,' sezee, 'sell him some'rs outen dis naberhood, kase he done bin yer too long now,' sezee. 'No longer'n day 'fo' yistiddy,' sezee, 'Brer Fox pass me on de road, en whatter you reckin he say?' sezee:

"'Law, Brer Tarrypin,' sez Miss Meadows, sez she, 'you don't mean ter say he cust?' sez she, en den de gals hilt der fans up 'fo' der faces.

"'Oh, no, ma'm,' sez Brer Tarrypin, sezee, 'he didn't cust, but he holler out—"Heyo, Stinkin' Jim!"'" sezee.

"'Oh, my! You hear dat, gals?' sez Miss Meadows, sez she; 'Brer Fox call Brer Tarrypin Stinkin'

Jim,' sez she, en den Miss Meadows en de gals make great wonderment how Brer Fox kin talk dat a way 'bout nice man like Brer Tarrypin.

" But bless grashus, honey ! w'ilst all dis gwine on, Brer Fox wuz stannin' at de back do' wid one year at de cat-hole lissenin'.   Eave-drappers don't hear no good er deyse'f, en de way Brer Fox wuz 'bused dat day wuz a caution.

" Bimeby Brer Fox stick his head in de do', en holler out :

" ' Good evenin', fokes, I wish you mighty well,' sezee, en wid dat he make a dash for Brer Rabbit, but Miss Meadows en de gals dey holler en squall, dey did,

en Brer Tarrypin he got ter scramblin' roun' up dar on de shelf, en off he come, en blip he tuck Brer Fox

on de back er de head. Dis sorter stunted Brer Fox,
en w'en he gedder his 'membunce de mos' he seed wuz
a pot er greens turnt over in de fireplace, en a broke
cheer. Brer Rabbit wuz gone, en Brer Tarrypin wuz
gone, en Miss Meadows en de gals wuz gone."

" Where did the Rabbit go, Uncle Remus ? " the
little boy asked, after a pause.

" Bless yo' soul, honey ! Brer Rabbit he skint up
de chimbly—dats w'at turnt de pot er greens over.
Brer Tarrypin, he crope under de bed, he did, en got
behime de cloze-chist, en Miss Meadows en de gals, dey
run out in de yard.

" Brer Fox, he sorter look roun' en feel er de back
er his head, whar Brer Tarrypin lit, but he don't see
no sine er Brer Rabbit. But de smoke en de ashes
gwine up de chimbly got de best er Brer Rabbit, en
bimeby he sneeze—*huckychow !*

" ' Aha ! ' sez Brer Fox, sezee ; ' youer dar, is you ? '
sezee. ' Well, I'm gwineter smoke you out, ef it takes
a mont'. Youer mine dis time,' sezee. Brer Rabbit
ain't sayin' nuthin'.

" ' Ain't you comin' down ? ' sez Brer Fox, sezee.
Brer Rabbit ain't sayin' nuthin'. Den Brer Fox, he
went out atter some wood, he did, en w'en he come
back he hear Brer Rabbit laughin'.

" ' W'at you laughin' at, Brer Rabbit ? ' sez Brer
Fox, sezee.

" ' Can't tell you, Brer Fox,' sez Brer Rabbit, sezee.

" ' Better tell, Brer Rabbit,' sez Brer Fox, sezee.

" ' 'Tain't nuthin' but a box er money somebody done gone en lef' up yer in de chink er de chimbly,' sez Brer Rabbit, sezee.

" ' Don't b'leeve you,' sez Brer Fox, sezee.

" ' Look up en see,' sez Brer Rabbit, sezee, en w'en Brer Fox look up, Brer Rabbit spit his eyes full er

terbarker joose, he did, en Brer Fox, he make a break fer de branch, en Brer Rabbitt he come down en tole de ladies good-by.

" 'How you git 'im off, Brer Rabbit?' sez Miss Meadows, sez she.

" ' Who ? me ?' sez Brer Rabbit, sezee ; ' w'y I des
tuck en tole 'im dat ef he didn't go 'long home en stop
playin' his pranks on spectubble fokes, dat I'd take 'im
out and th'ash 'im,' sezee."

" And what became of the Terrapin ? " asked the
little boy.

" Oh, well den ! " exclaimed the old man, " chilluns
can't speck ter know all 'bout eve'ything 'fo' dey git
some res'. Dem eyeleds er yone wanter be propped
wid straws dis minnit."

XI.

MR. WOLF MAKES A FAILURE.

" I LAY yo' ma got comp'ny," said Uncle Remus, as
the little boy entered the old man's door with a huge
piece of mince-pie in his hand, " en ef she ain't got
comp'ny, den she done gone en drap de cubberd key
som'ers whar you done run up wid it."

" Well, I saw the pie lying there, Uncle Remus,
and I just thought I'd fetch it out to you."

" Tooby sho, honey," replied the old man, regarding the child with admiration. " Tooby sho, honey ;
dat changes marters. Chrismus doin's is outer date, en
dey ain't got no bizness layin' roun' loose. Dish yer
pie," Uncle Remus continued, holding it up and meas-
uring it with an experienced eye, " will gimme strenk

fer ter persoo on atter Brer Fox en Brer Rabbit en de
udder creeturs w'at dey roped in 'long wid um."

Here the old man paused, and proceeded to demol-
ish the pie—a feat accomplished in a very short time.
Then he wiped the crumbs from his beard and began :

" Brer Fox feel so bad, en he git so mad 'bout Brer
Rabbit, dat he dunner w'at ter do, en he look mighty
down-hearted. Bimeby, one day wiles he wuz gwine
'long de road, old Brer Wolf come up wid 'im. W'en
dey done howdyin' en axin' atter one nudder's fambly
connexshun, Brer Wolf, he 'low, he did, dat der wuz
sump'n wrong wid Brer Fox, en Brer Fox, he 'low'd
der wern't, en he went on en laugh en make great ter-
do kaze Brer Wolf look like he spishun sump'n. But
Brer Wolf, he got mighty long head, en he sorter
broach 'bout Brer Rabbit's kyar'ns on, kaze de way dat
Brer Rabbit 'ceive Brer Fox done got ter be de talk er
de naberhood. Den Brer Fox en Brer Wolf dey
sorter palavered on, dey did, twel bimeby Brer Wolf
he up'n say dat he done got plan fix fer ter trap Brer
Rabbit. Den Brer Fox say how. Den Brer Wolf
up'n tell 'im dat de way fer ter git de drap on Brer
Rabbit wuz ter git 'im in Brer Fox house. Brer Fox
dun know Brer Rabbit uv ole, en he know dat sorter
game done wo' ter a frazzle, but Brer Wolf, he talk
mighty 'swadin'.

" 'How you gwine git 'im dar ?' sez Brer Fox,
sezee.

" ' Fool 'im dar,' sez Brer Wolf, sezee.

" ' Who gwine do de foolin' ? ' sez Brer Fox, sezee.

" ' I'll do de foolin',' sez Brer Wolf, sezee, ' ef you'll do de gamin',' sezee.

" ' How you gwine do it ? ' sez Brer Fox, sezee.

" ' You run 'long home, en git on de bed, en make like you dead, en don't you say nothin' twel Brer Rabbit come en put his han's onter you,' sez Brer Wolf, sezee, ' en ef we don't git 'im fer supper, Joe's dead en Sal's a widder,' sezee.

"Dis look like mighty nice game, en Brer Fox 'greed. So den he amble off home, en Brer Wolf, he march off ter Brer Rabbit house. W'en he got dar, hit look like nobody at home, but Brer Wolf he walk up en knock on de do'—blam! blam! Nobody come. Den he lam aloose en knock 'gin—blim! blim!

" 'Who dar?' sez Brer Rabbit, sezee.

" 'Fr'en',' sez Brer Wolf.

" 'Too menny fr'en's spiles de dinner,' sez Brer Rabbit, sezee; 'w'ich un's dis?' sezee.

" 'I fetch bad news, Brer Rabbit,' sez Brer Wolf, sezee.

" 'Bad news is soon tole,' sez Brer Rabbit, sezee.

"By dis time Brer Rabbit done come ter de do', wid his head tied up in a red hankcher.

" 'Brer Fox died dis mornin',' sez Brer Wolf, sezee.

" 'Whar yo' mo'nin' gown, Brer Wolf?' sez Brer Rabbit, sezee.

" 'Gwine atter it now,' sez Brer Wolf, sezee. 'I des call by fer ter bring de news. I went down ter Brer Fox house little bit 'go, en dar I foun' 'im stiff,' sezee.

"Den Brer Wolf lope off. Brer Rabbit sot down en scratch his head, he did, en bimeby he say ter hisse'f dat he b'leeve he sorter drap 'roun' by Brer Fox house fer ter see how de lan' lay. No sooner said'n done. Up he jump, en out he went. W'en Brer Rabbit got

close ter Brer Fox house, all look lonesome. Den he
went up nigher. Nobody stirrin'. Den he look in,
en dar lay Brer Fox stretch out on de bed des ez big

ez life. Den Brer Rabbit make like he talkin' to
hisse'f.

"'Nobody 'roun' fer ter look atter Brer Fox—not
even Brer Tukkey Buzzard ain't come ter de funer'l,'
sezee. 'I hope Brer Fox ain't dead, but I speck he is,'
sezee. 'Even down ter Brer Wolf done gone en lef'
'im. Hit's de busy season wid me, but I'll set up wid
'im. He seem like he dead, yit he mayn't be,' sez
Brer Rabbit, sezee. 'W'en a man go ter see dead
fokes, dead fokes allers raises up der behime leg en
hollers, *wahoo!*' sezee.

"Brer Fox he stay still.   Den Brer Rabbit he talk
little louder:

"'Mighty funny.   Brer Fox look like he dead, yit
he don't do like he dead.   Dead fokes hists der behime
leg en hollers *wahoo!* w'en a man come ter see um,'
sez Brer Rabbit, sezee.

"Sho' nuff, Brer Fox lif' up his foot en holler
wahoo! en Brer Rabbit he tear out de house like de
dogs wuz atter 'im.   Brer Wolf mighty smart, but
nex' time you hear fum 'im, honey, he'll be in trouble.
You des hole yo' breff'n wait."

XII.

MR. FOX TACKLES OLD MAN TARRYPIN.

"ONE day," said Uncle Remus, sharpening his knife
on the palm of his hand—" one day Brer Fox strike up
wid Brer Tarrypin right in de middle er de big road.
Brer Tarrypin done heerd 'im comin', en he 'low ter
hissef dat he'd sorter keep one eye open; but Brer Fox
wuz monstus perlite, en he open up de confab, he did,
like he ain't see Brer Tarrypin sence de las' freshit.

"'Heyo, Brer Tarrypin, whar you bin dis long-
come-short?' sez Brer Fox, sezee.

"'Lounjun 'roun', Brer Fox, lounjun 'roun',' sez
Brer Tarrypin.

" ' You don't look sprucy like you did, Brer Tarry-pin,' sez Brer Fox, sezee.

" ' Lounjun 'roun' en suffer'n',' sez Brer Tarrypin, sezee.

" Den de talk sorter run on like dis:

" ' W'at ail you, Brer Tarrypin? Yo' eye look mighty red,' sez Brer Fox, sezee.

" ' Lor', Brer Fox, you dunner w'at trubble is. You ain't bin lounjun 'roun' en suffer'n',' sez Brer Tarrypin, sezee.

" ' Bofe eyes red, en you look like you mighty weak, Brer Tarrypin,' sez Brer Fox, sezee.

" ' Lor', Brer Fox, you dunner w'at trubble is,' sez Brer Tarrypin, sezee.

" ' W'at ail you now, Brer Tarrypin?' sez Brer Fox, sezee.

" 'Tuck a walk de udder day, en man come 'long en sot de fiel' a-fier. Lor', Brer Fox, you dunner w'at trubble is,' sez Brer Tarrypin, sezee.

" ' How you git out de fier, Brer Tarrypin?' sez Brer Fox, sezee.

" ' Sot en tuck it, Brer Fox,' sez Brer Tarrypin, sezee. 'Sot en tuck it, en de smoke sif' in my eye, en de fier scorch my back,' sez Brer Tarrypin, sezee.

" ' Likewise hit bu'n yo' tail off,' sez Brer Fox, sezee.

" ' Oh, no, dar's de tail, Brer Fox,' sez Brer Tarrypin, sezee, en wid dat he oncurl his tail fum under de shell, en no sooner did he do dat dan Brer Fox grab it, en holler out:

" ' Oh, yes, Brer Tarrypin! Oh, yes! En so youer de man w'at lam me on de head at Miss Meadows's is you? Youer in wid Brer Rabbit, is you? Well, I'm gwineter out you.'

" Brer Tarrypin beg en beg, but 'twan't no use. Brer Fox done been fool so much dat he look like he 'termin' fer ter have Brer Tarrypin haslett. Den Brer Tarrypin beg Brer Fox not fer ter drown 'im, but Brer Fox ain't makin' no prommus, en den he beg Brer Fox fer ter bu'n' 'im, kase he done useter fier, but Brer Fox don't say nuthin'. Bimeby Brer Fox drag Brer Tarrypin off little ways b'low de spring-'ouse, en souze 'im under de water. Den Brer Tarrypin begin fer ter holler:

" ' Tu'n loose dat stump root en ketch holt er me—
tu'n loose dat stump root en ketch holt er me.'

" Brer Fox he holler back :

" ' I ain't got holt er no stump root, en I is got holt
er you.'

" Brer Tarrypin he keep on holler'n :

" ' Ketch holt er me—I'm a drownin'—I'm a drownin'—tu'n loose de stump root en ketch holt er me.'

" Sho nuff, Brer Fox tu'n loose de tail, en Brer Tarrypin, he went down ter de bottom—kerblunkity-blink ! "

No typographical combination or description could do justice to the guttural sonorousness—the peculiar intonation—which Uncle Remus imparted to this combination. It was so peculiar, indeed, that the little boy asked :

" How did he go to the bottom, Uncle Remus ? "

" Kerblunkity-blink ! "

" Was he drowned, Uncle Remus ? "

" Who ? Ole man Tarrypin ? Is you drowndid w'en yo' ma tucks you in de bed ? "

" Well, no," replied the little boy, dubiously.

" Ole man Tarrypin wuz at home I tell you, honey. Kerblinkity-blunk ! "

XIII.

THE AWFUL FATE OF MR. WOLF.

UNCLE REMUS was half-soling one of his shoes, and his Miss Sally's little boy had been handling his awls, his hammers, and his knives to such an extent that the old man was compelled to assume a threatening attitude; but peace reigned again, and the little boy perched himself on a chair, watching Uncle Remus driving in pegs.

"Folks w'at's allers pesterin' people, en bodderin' 'longer dat w'at ain't dern, don't never come ter no good eend. Dar wuz Brer Wolf; stidder mindin' un his own bizness, he hatter take en go in pardnerships wid Brer Fox, en dey want skacely a minnit in de day dat he want atter Brer Rabbit, en he kep' on en kep' on twel fus' news you knowed he got kotch up wid— en he got kotch up wid monstus bad."

"Goodness, Uncle Remus! I thought the Wolf let the Rabbit alone, after he tried to fool him about the Fox being dead."

"Better lemme tell dish yer my way. Bimeby hit'll be yo' bed time, en Miss Sally'll be a hollerin' atter you, en you'll be a whimplin' roun', en den Mars John'll fetch up de re'r wid dat ar strop w'at I made fer 'im."

The child laughed, and playfully shook his fist in the simple, serious face of the venerable old darkey, but said no more. Uncle Remus waited awhile to be sure there was to be no other demonstration, and then proceeded :

"Brer Rabbit ain't see no peace w'atsumever. He can't leave home 'cep' Brer Wolf 'ud make a raid en tote off some er de fambly. Brer Rabbit b'ilt 'im a

straw house, en hit wuz tored down; den he made a
house outen pine-tops, en dat went de same way; den

he made 'im a bark house, en dat wuz raided on, en
eve'y time he los' a house he los' one er his chilluns.
Las' Brer Rabbit got mad, he did, en cust, en den he
went off, he did, en got some kyarpinters, en dey b'ilt
'im a plank house wid rock foundashuns. Atter dat
he could have some peace en quietness. He could go
out en pass de time er day wid his neighbors, en come
back en set by de fier, en smoke his pipe, en read de
newspapers same like enny man w'at got a fambly.
He made a hole, he did, in de cellar whar de little
Rabbits could hide out w'en dar wuz much uv a racket

in de neighborhood, en de latch er de front do' kotch on
de inside. Brer Wolf, he see how de lan' lay, he did,
en he lay low. De little Rabbits was mighty skittish,
but hit got so dat cole chills ain't run up Brer Rabbit's
back no mo' w'en he heerd Brer Wolf go gallopin' by.

"Bimeby, one day w'en Brer Rabbit wuz fixin' fer
ter call on Miss Coon, he heerd a monstus fuss en clat-
ter up de big road, en 'mos' 'fo' he could fix his years
fer ter lissen, Brer Wolf run in de do'. De little Rabbits dey went inter dere hole in de cellar, dey did, like
blowin' out a cannle. Brer Wolf wuz far'ly kivver'd
wid mud, en mighty nigh outer win'.

"'Oh, do pray save me, Brer Rabbit!' sez Brer
Wolf, sezee. 'Do please, Brer Rabbit! de dogs is
atter me, en dey'll t'ar me up. Don't you year um
comin'? Oh, do please save me, Brer Rabbit! Hide
me some'rs whar de dogs won't git me.'

"No quicker sed dan done.

"'Jump in dat big chist dar, Brer Wolf,' sez Brer
Rabbit, sezee; 'jump in dar en make yo'se'f at home.'

"In jump Brer Wolf, down come the led, en inter
de hasp went de hook, en dar Mr. Wolf wuz. Den
Brer Rabbit went ter de lookin'-glass, he did, en wink
at hisse'f, en den he draw'd de rockin'-cheer in front er
de fier, he did, en tuck a big chaw terbarker."

"Tobacco, Uncle Remus?" asked the little boy, in-
credulously.

"Rabbit terbarker, honey. You know dis yer life

ev'lastin' w'at Miss Sally puts 'mong de cloze in de
trunk ; well, dat's rabbit terbarker. Den Brer Rabbit
sot dar long time, he did, turnin' his mine over en
wukken his thinkin' masheen.

Bimeby he got up, en sor-
ter stir 'roun'. Den
Brer Wolf open up :

"'Is de dogs
all gone, Brer
Rabbit ?'

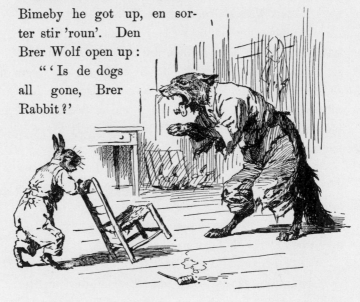

"'Seem like I hear one un um smellin' roun' de
chimbly-cornder des now.'

"Den Brer Rabbit git de kittle en fill it full er
water, en put it on de fier.

"'W'at you doin' now, Brer Rabbit ?'

"'I'm fixin' fer ter make you a nice cup er tea,
Brer Wolf.'

"Den Brer Rabbit went ter de cubberd en git de

gimlet, en commence for ter bo' little holes in de chist-
led.

" ' W'at you doin' now, Brer Rabbit ? '

" ' I'm a bo'in'
little holes so you
kin get bref, Brer
Wolf.'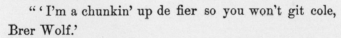

" Den Brer Rab-
bit went out en git
some mo' wood, en
fling it on de fier.

" ' W'at you doin'
now, Brer Rabbit ? '

" ' I'm a chunkin' up de fier so you won't git cole,
Brer Wolf.'

" Den Brer Rabbit went down inter de cellar en
fotch out all his chilluns.

" ' W'at you doin' now, Brer Rabbit ? '

" ' I'm a tellin' my chilluns w'at a nice man you is,
Brer Wolf.'

" En de chilluns, dey had ter put der han's on der
moufs fer ter keep fum laffin'.   Den Brer Rabbit he
got de kittle en commenced fer to po' de hot water on
de chist-lid.

" ' W'at dat I hear, Brer Rabbit ? '

" ' You hear de win' a blowin', Brer Wolf.'

" Den de water begin fer ter sif' thoo.

" ' W'at dat I feel, Brer Rabbit ? '

" ' You feels de fleas a bitin', Brer Wolf.'

" ' Dey er bitin' mighty hard, Brer Rabbit.'

" ' Tu'n over on de udder side, Brer Wolf.'

" ' W'at dat I feel now, Brer Rabbit ? '

" ' Still you feels de fleas, Brer Wolf.'

" ' Dey er eatin' me up, Brer Rabbit,' en dem wuz de las' words er Brer Wolf, kase de scaldin' water done de bizness.

" Den Brer Rabbit call in his neighbors, he did, en dey hilt a reg'lar juberlee; en ef you go ter Brer Rabbit's house right now, I dunno but w'at you'll fine Brer Wolf's hide hangin' in de back-po'ch, en all bekaze he wuz so bizzy wid udder fo'kses doin's."

XIV.

MR. FOX AND THE DECEITFUL FROGS.

WHEN the little boy ran in to see Uncle Remus the night after he had told him of the awful fate of Brer Wolf, the only response to his greeting was:

" I-doom-er-ker-kum-mer-ker ! "

No explanation could convey an adequate idea of the intonation and pronunciation which Uncle Remus brought to bear upon this wonderful word. Those who can recall to mind the peculiar gurgling, jerking, liquid sound made by pouring water from a large jug, or the

sound produced by throwing several stones in rapid
succession into a pond of deep water, may be able to
form a very faint idea of the sound, but it can not be
reproduced in print. The little boy was astonished.

"What did you say, Uncle Remus?"

"I-doom-er-ker-kum-mer-ker! I-doom-er-ker-kum-
mer-ker!"

"What is that?"

"Dat's Tarrypin talk, dat is. Bless yo' soul, honey,"
continued the old man, brightening up, "w'en you git
ole ez me—w'en you see w'at I sees, en year w'at I
years—de creeturs dat you can't talk wid 'll be mighty
skase—dey will dat. W'y, ders er old gray rat w'at
uses 'bout yer, en time atter time he comes out w'en
you all done gone ter bed en sets up dar in de cornder
en dozes, en me en him talks by de 'our; en w'at dat
old rat dunno ain't down in de spellin' book. Des now,
w'en you run in and broke me up, I wuz fetchin' inter
my mine w'at Brer Tarrypin say ter Brer Fox w'en he
turn 'im loose in de branch."

"What did he say, Uncle Remus?"

"Dat w'at he said—I-doom-er-ker-kum-mer-ker!
Brer Tarrypin wuz at de bottom er de pon', en he talk
back, he did, in bubbles—I-doom-er-ker-kum-mer-ker!
Brer Fox, he ain't sayin' nuthin', but Brer Bull-Frog,
settin' on de bank, he hear Brer Tarrypin, he did, en
he holler back:

"'Jug-er-rum-kum-dum! Jug-er-rum-kum-dum!'

" Den n'er Frog holler out :

" ' Knee-deep !   Knee-deep ! '

" Den ole Brer Bull - Frog, **he** holler back :

" ' Don't - you-ber-lieve-'im ! Don't-you-berlieve-'im ! '

" Den de bubbles **come** up fum Brer Tarrypin :

" ' I-doom-er-ker-kum-mer-ker ! '

" Den n'er Frog sing out :

" ' Wade in !   Wade in ! '

" Den ole Brer Bull-Frog talk thoo his ho'seness :

" ' Dar-you'll-fine-yo'-brudder !   Dar-you'll-fine-yo'-brudder ! '

" Sho nuff, Brer Fox look over de bank, he did, en dar wuz n'er Fox lookin' at 'im outer de water.   Den

he retch out fer ter shake han's, en in he went, heels
over head, en Brer Tarrypin bubble out:

"'I-doom-er-ker-kum-mer-ker!'"

"Was the Fox drowned, Uncle Remus?" asked the
little boy.

"He wern't zackly drowndid, honey," replied the

old man, with an air of cautious reserve. "He did manage fer ter scramble out, but a little mo' en de Mud Turkle would er got 'im, en den he'd er bin made hash un worril widout een'."

XV.

MR. FOX GOES A-HUNTING, BUT MR. RABBIT BAGS THE GAME.

"ATTER Brer Fox hear 'bout how Brer Rabbit done Brer Wolf," said Uncle Remus, scratching his head with the point of his awl, " he 'low, he did, dat he better not be so brash, en he sorter let Brer Rabbit 'lone. Dey wuz all time seein' one nudder, en 'bunnunce er times Brer Fox could er nab Brer Rabbit, but eve'y time he got de chance, his mine 'ud sorter rezume 'bout Brer Wolf, en he let Brer Rabbit 'lone. Bimeby dey 'gun ter git kinder familious wid wunner nudder like dey useter, en it got so Brer Fox'd call on Brer Rabbit, en dey'd set up en smoke der pipes, dey would, like no ha'sh feelin's 'd ever rested 'twixt um.

"Las', one day Brer Fox come 'long all rig out, en ax Brer Rabbit fer ter go huntin' wid 'im, but Brer Rabbit, he sorter feel lazy, en he tell Brer Fox dat he got some udder fish fer ter fry. Brer Fox feel mighty sorry, he did, but he say he b'leeve he try his

han' enny how, en off he put. He wuz gone all day,
en he had a monstus streak er luck, Brer Fox did, en
he bagged a sight er game. Bime-
by, to'rds de shank er de evenin',
Brer Rabbit sorter stretch hisse'f,
he did, en 'low hit's mos' time fer

Brer Fox fer ter git 'long home. Den Brer Rabbit,
he went'n mounted a stump fer ter see ef he could
year Brer Fox comin'. He ain't bin dar long, twel
sho' nuff, yer come Brer Fox thoo de woods, singing
like a nigger at a frolic. Brer Rabbit, he lipt down
off'n de stump, he did, en lay down in de road en
make like he dead. Brer Fox he come 'long, he did,
en see Brer Rabbit layin' dar. He tu'n 'im over, he
did, en 'zamine 'im, en say, sezee :

"'Dish yer rabbit dead. He look like he bin

dead long time. He dead, but he mighty fat. He de fattes' rabbit w'at I ever see, but he bin dead too long. I feard ter take 'im home,' sezee.

"Brer Rabbit ain't sayin' nuthin'. Brer Fox, he sorter lick his chops, but he went on en lef' Brer Rabbit layin' in de road. Dreckly he wuz outer sight, Brer Rabbit, he jump up, he did, en run roun' thoo de woods en git befo Brer Fox agin. Brer Fox, he come up, en dar lay Brer Rabbit, periently cole en stiff. Brer Fox, he look at Brer Rabbit, en he sorter study. At-

ter while he onslung his game-bag, en say ter hisse'f, sezee :

" ' Deze yer rabbits gwine ter was'e. I'll des 'bout leave my game yer, en I'll go back'n git dat udder rabbit, en I'll make fokes b'leeve dat I'm ole man Hunter fum Huntsville,' sezee.

"En wid dat he drapt his game en loped back up de road atter de udder rabbit, en w'en he got outer sight, ole Brer Rabbit, he snatch up Brer Fox game en put out fer home. Nex' time he see Brer Fox, he holler out :

"'What you kill de udder day, Brer Fox?' sezee.

"Den Brer Fox, he sorter koam his flank wid his tongue, en holler back :

"'I kotch a han'ful er hard sense, Brer Rabbit,' sezee.

"Den ole Brer Rabbit, he laff, he did, en up en 'spon', sezee :

"'Ef I'd a know'd you wuz atter dat, Brer Fox, I'd a loant you some er mine,' sezee."

XVI.

OLD MR. RABBIT, HE'S A GOOD FISHERMAN.

"Brer Rabbit en Brer Fox wuz like some chilluns w'at I knows un," said Uncle Remus, regarding the little boy, who had come to hear another story, with an affectation of great solemnity. "Bofe un um wuz allers atter wunner nudder, a prankin' en a pester'n 'roun', but Brer Rabbit did had some peace, kaze Brer Fox done got skittish 'bout puttin' de clamps on Brer Rabbit.

"One day, w'en Brer Rabbit, en Brer Fox, en Brer Coon, en Brer B'ar, en a whole lot un um wuz clearin' up a new groun' fer ter plant a roas'n'year patch, de sun 'gun ter git sorter hot, en Brer Rabbit he got tired ; but he didn't let on, kaze he 'fear'd de balance un um'd call 'im lazy, en he keep on totin' off trash en pilin' up bresh, twel bimeby he holler out dat he gotter brier in his han', en den he take'n slip off, en hunt fer cool place fer

ter res'. Atter w'ile he come 'crosst a well wid a bucket hangin' in it.

" 'Dat look cool,' sez Brer Rabbit, sezee, 'en cool I speck she is. I'll des 'bout git in dar en take a nap,' en wid dat in he jump, he did, en he ain't no sooner fix hisse'f dan de bucket 'gun ter go down."

"Wasn't the Rabbit scared, Uncle Remus?" asked the little boy.

" Honey, dey ain't been no wusser skeer'd beas'
sence de worril begin dan dish yer same Brer Rabbit.
He fa'rly had a ager. He know whar he cum fum, but
he dunner whar he gwine. Dreckly he feel de bucket
hit de water, en dar she sot, but Brer Rabbit he keep
mighty still, kaze he dunner w'at minnit gwineter be
de nex'. He des lay dar en shuck en shiver.

" Brer Fox allers got one eye on Brer Rabbit, en
w'en he slip off fum de new groun', Brer Fox he sneak
atter 'im. He know Brer Rabbit wuz atter some
projick er nudder, en he tuck'n crope off, he did, en
watch 'im. Brer Fox see Brer Rabbit come to de well
en stop, en den he see 'im jump in de bucket, en
den, lo en beholes, he see 'im go down outer sight.
Brer Fox wuz de mos' 'stonish Fox dat you ever laid
eyes on. He sot off dar in de bushes en study en
study, but he don't make no head ner tails ter dis
kinder bizness. Den he say ter hisse'f, sezee :

" 'Well, ef dis don't bang my times,' sezee, ' den
Joe's dead en Sal's a widder. Right down dar in dat
well Brer Rabbit keep his money hid, en ef 'tain't dat
den he done gone en 'skiver'd a gole-mine, en ef
'tain't dat, den I'm a gwineter see w'at's in dar,'
sezee.

" Brer Fox crope up little nigher, he did, en lissen,
but he don't year no fuss, en he keep on gittin' nigher,
en yit he don't year nuthin'. Bimeby he git up close
en peep down, but he don't see nuthin' en he don't

year nuthin'. All dis time Brer Rabbit mighty nigh
skeer'd outen his skin, en he fear'd fer ter move kaze
de bucket might keel over en spill him out in de
water. W'ile he sayin' his pra'rs over like a train er
kyars runnin', ole Brer Fox holler out:

"'Heyo, Brer Rabbit! Who you wizzitin' down
dar?' sezee.

"'Who? Me? Oh, I'm des a fishin', Brer Fox,'
sez Brer Rabbit, sezee. 'I des say ter myse'f dat I'd
sorter sprize you all wid a mess er fishes fer dinner,
en so here I is, en dar's de fishes. I'm a fishin' fer
suckers, Brer Fox,' sez Brer Rabbit, sezee.

"'Is dey many un um down dar, Brer Rabbit?'
sez Brer Fox, sezee.

"'Lots un um, Brer Fox; scoze en scoze un um.
De water is natally live wid um. Come down en
he'p me haul um in, Brer Fox,' sez Brer Rabbit,
sezee.

"'How I gwineter git down, Brer Rabbit?'

"'Jump inter de bucket, Brer Fox. Hit'll fetch
you down all safe en soun'.'

"Brer Rabbit talk so happy en talk so sweet dat
Brer Fox he jump in de bucket, he did, en, ez he
went down, co'se his weight pull Brer Rabbit up.
W'en dey pass one nudder on de half-way groun',
Brer Rabbit he sing out:

"'Good-by, Brer Fox, take keer yo' cloze,
Fer dis-is de way de worril goes;

Some goes up en some goes down,
You'll git ter de bottom all safe en soun'.' *

"W'en Brer Rabbit got out, he gallop off en tole de fokes w'at de well b'long ter dat Brer Fox wuz down in dar mud-dyin' up de drinkin' water, en den he gallop back ter de well, en holler down ter Brer Fox:

"'Yer come a man wid a great big gun— W'en he haul you up, you jump en run.'"

"What then, Uncle Remus?" asked the little boy, as the old man paused.

"In des 'bout half n'our, honey, bofe un um wuz back in de new groun' wukkin des like dey never heer'd er no well, ceppin' dat eve'y now'n den Brer Rabbit'd bust out in er laff, en ole Brer Fox, he'd git a spell er de dry grins."

---

* As a Northern friend suggests that this story may be somewhat obscure, it may be as well to state that the well is supposed to be supplied with a rope over a wheel, or pulley, with a bucket at each end.

XVII.

MR. RABBIT NIBBLES UP THE BUTTER.

"DE animils en de creeturs," said Uncle Remus,
shaking his coffee around in the bottom of his tin-cup,
in order to gather up all the sugar, "dey kep' on gittin' mo' en mo' familious wid wunner nudder, twel
bimeby, 'twan't long 'fo' Brer Rabbit, en Brer Fox,
en Brer Possum got ter sorter bunchin' der perwishuns
tergedder in de same shanty.   Atter w'ile de roof
sorter 'gun ter leak, en one day Brer Rabbit, en Brer
Fox, en Brer Possum, 'semble fer ter see ef dey can't
kinder patch her up.   Dey had a big day's work in
front un um, en dey fotch der dinner wid um.   Dey
lump de vittles up in one pile, en de butter w'at Brer
Fox brung, dey goes en puts in de spring-'ouse fer ter
keep cool, en den dey went ter wuk, en 'twan't long
'fo' Brer Rabbit stummuck 'gun ter sorter growl en
pester 'im.   Dat butter er Brer Fox sot heavy on his
mine, en his mouf water eve'y time he 'member 'bout
it.   Present'y he say ter hisse'f dat he bleedzd ter have
a nip at dat butter, en den he lay his plans, he did.
Fus' news you know, w'ile dey wuz all wukkin' 'long,
Brer Rabbit raise his head quick en fling his years
forrerd en holler out:

"'Here I is.   W'at you want wid me?' en off
he put like sump'n wuz atter 'im.

"He sallied 'roun', ole Brer Rabbit did, en atter he make sho dat nobody ain't foller'n un 'im, inter de spring-'ouse he bounces, en dar he stays twel he git a bait er butter. Den he santer on back en go to wuk.

"'Whar you bin?' sez Brer Fox, sezee.

"'I hear my chilluns callin' me,' sez Brer Rabbit, sezee, 'en I hatter go see w'at dey want. My ole 'oman done gone en tuck mighty sick,' sezee.

"Dey wuk on twel bimeby de butter tas'e so good dat ole Brer Rabbit want some mo'. Den he raise up his head, he did, en holler out:

"'Heyo! Hole on! I'm a comin'!' en off he put.

"Dis time he stay right smart w'ile, en w'en he git back Brer Fox ax him whar he bin.

"'I been ter see my ole 'oman, en she's a sinkin',' sezee.

"Dreckly Brer Rabbit hear um callin' 'im ag'in en off he goes, en dis time, bless yo' soul, he gits de butter out so clean dat he kin see hisse'f in de bottom er de

bucket. He scrape it clean en lick it dry, en den he
go back ter wuk lookin' mo' samer dan a nigger w'at
de patter-rollers bin had holt un.

"'How's yo' ole 'oman dis time?' sez Brer Fox,
sezee.

"'I'm oblije ter you, Brer Fox,' sez Brer Rabbit,
sezee, 'but I'm fear'd she's done gone by now,' en dat
sorter make Brer Fox en Brer Possum feel in moanin'
wid Brer Rabbit.

"Bimeby, w'en dinner-time come, dey all got out
der vittles, but Brer Rabbit keep on lookin' lonesome,
en Brer Fox en Brer Possum dey sorter rustle roun'
fer ter see ef dey can't make Brer Rabbit feel sorter
splimmy."

"What is that, Uncle Remus?" asked the little
boy.

"Sorter splimmy-splammy, honey—sorter like he
in a crowd—sorter like his ole 'oman ain't dead ez she
mout be. You know how fokes duz w'en dey gits
whar people's a moanin'."

The little boy didn't know, fortunately for him,
and Uncle Remus went on:

"Brer Fox en Brer Possum rustle roun', dey did,
gittin out de vittles, en bimeby Brer Fox, he say,
sezee :

"'Brer Possum, you run down ter de spring en
fetch de butter, en I'll sail 'roun' yer en set de table,'
sezee.

"Brer Possum, he lope off atter de butter, en dreckly here he come lopin' back wid his years a trimblin' en his tongue a hangin' out. Brer Fox, he holler out :

" ' W'at de matter now, Brer Possum ? ' sezee.

" ' You all better run yer, fokes,' sez Brer Possum, sezee. ' De las' drap er dat butter done gone ! '

" ' Whar she gone ? ' sez Brer Fox, sezee.

" ' Look like she dry up,' sez Brer Possum, sezee.

" Den Brer Rabbit, he look sorter sollum, he did, en he up'n say, sezee.

" ' I speck dat butter melt in somebody mouf,' sezee.

" Den dey went down ter de spring wid Brer Pos-sum, en sho nuff de butter done gone. W'iles dey wuz sputin' over der wunderment, Brer Rabbit say he see tracks all 'roun' dar, en he p'int out dat ef dey'll all go ter sleep, he kin ketch de chap w'at stole de butter. Den dey all lie down en Brer Fox en Brer Possum dey soon drapt off ter sleep, but Brer Rabbit he stay 'wake, en w'en de time come he raise up easy en smear Brer Possum mouf wid de butter on his paws, en den he run off en nibble up de bes' er de dinner w'at dey lef' layin' out, en den he come back en wake up Brer Fox, en show 'im de butter on Brer Possum mouf. Den dey wake up Brer Possum, en tell 'im 'bout it, but c'ose Brer Possum 'ny it ter de las'. Brer Fox, dough, he's a kinder lawyer, en he

argafy dis way—dat Brer Possum wuz de fus one at
de butter, en de fus one fer ter miss it, en mo'n dat,
dar hang de signs on his mouf. Brer Pos-
sum see dat dey
got 'im jammed up

in a cornder, en
den he up en say
dat de way fer ter
ketch de man w'at
stole de butter is ter b'il' a big bresh-heap en set her
afier, en all han's try ter jump over, en de one w'at
fall in, den he de chap w'at stole de butter. Brer
Rabbit en Brer Fox dey bofe 'gree, dey did, en dey
whirl in en b'il' de bresh-heap, en dey b'il' her high en
dey b'il' her wide, en den dey totch her off. W'en she
got ter blazin' up good, Brer Rabbit, he tuck de fus
turn. He sorter step back, en look 'roun' en giggle,

en over he went mo' samer dan a bird flyin'. Den
come Brer Fox. He got back little fudder, en spit
on his han's, en lit out en made de jump, en he come
so nigh gittin' in dat
de een' er his tail
kotch afier. Ain't you

never see no fox,
honey?" inquired
Uncle Remus, in
a tone that implied both conciliation and information.

The little boy thought probably he had, but he
wouldn't commit himself.

"Well, den," continued the old man, "nex' time
you see one un um, you look right close en see ef de
een' er his tail ain't w'ite. Hit's des like I tell you.
Dey b'ars de skyar er dat bresh-heap down ter dis day.
Dey er marked—dat's w'at dey is—dey er marked."

" And what about Brother Possum ? " asked the little boy.

" Ole Brer Possum, he tuck a runnin' start, he did, en he come lumberin' 'long, en he lit—kerblam !—right in de middle er de fier, en dat wuz de las' er ole Brer Possum."

" But, Uncle Remus, Brother Possum didn't steal the butter after all," said the little boy, who was not at all satisfied with such summary injustice.

" Dat w'at make I say w'at I duz, honey. In dis worril, lots er fokes is gotter suffer fer udder fokes sins. Look like hit's mighty onwrong ; but hit's des dat away. Tribbalashun seem like she's a waitin' roun' de cornder fer ter ketch one en all un us, honey."

XVIII.

MR. RABBIT FINDS HIS MATCH AT LAST.

" Hit look like ter me dat I let on de udder night dat in dem days w'en de creeturs wuz santer'n 'roun' same like fokes, none un um wuz brash nuff fer ter ketch up wid Brer Rabbit," remarked Uncle Remus, reflectively.

" Yes," replied the little boy, " that's what you said."

" Well, den," continued the old man with unction,

"dar's whar my 'membunce gin out, kaze Brer Rabbit
did git kotched up wid, en hit cool 'im off like po'in'
spring water on one er deze yer biggity fices."

"How was that, Uncle Remus?" asked the little
boy.

"One day w'en Brer Rabbit wuz gwine lippity-
clippitin' down de road, he meet up wid ole Brer
Tarrypin, en atter dey pass de time er day wid wunner
nudder, Brer Rabbit, he 'low dat he wuz much 'blije
ter Brer Tarrypin fer de han' he tuck in de rumpus
dat day down at Miss Meadows's."

"When he dropped off of the water-shelf on the
Fox's head," suggested the little boy.

"Dat's de same time, honey. Den Brer Tarrypin
'low dat Brer Fox run mighty fas' dat day,
but dat ef he'd er bin atter 'im stidder
Brer Rabbit, he'd er kotch 'im.   Brer
Rabbit say he could er kotch 'im hisse'f
but he didn't
keer 'bout leav-
in' de ladies.
Dey keep on
talkin', dey did,
twel   bimeby
dey gotter 'spu-
tin' 'bout w'ich
wuz de swif'es'.   Brer Rabbit, he say he kin outrun
Brer Tarrypin, en Brer Tarrypin, he des vow dat he

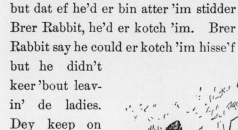

kin outrun Brer Rabbit. Up en down dey had it, twel
fus news you know Brer Tarrypin say he got a fifty-
dollar bill in de chink er de chimbly at home, en dat
bill done tole 'im dat he could beat Brer Rabbit in
a fa'r race. Den Brer Rabbit say he got a fifty-dol-
lar bill w'at say dat he kin leave Brer Tarrypin so fur
behime, dat he could sow barley ez he went 'long en
hit 'ud be ripe nuff fer ter cut by de time Brer Tarrypin pass dat way.

"Enny how dey make de bet en put up de money,
en ole Brer Tukky Buzzard, he wuz summonzd fer
ter be de jedge, en de stakeholder; en 'twan't long 'fo'
all de 'rangements wuz made. De race wuz a five-mile
heat, en de groun' wuz medjud off, en at de een' er
ev'ey mile a pos' wuz stuck up. Brer Rabbit wuz ter
run down de big road, en Brer Tarrypin, he say he'd
gallup thoo de woods. Fokes tole 'im he could git
long faster in de road, but ole Brer Tarrypin, he know
w'at he doin'. Miss Meadows en de gals en mos' all de
nabers got win' er de fun, en w'en de day wuz sot dey
'termin' fer ter be on han'. Brer Rabbit he train hisse'f ev'ey day, en he skip over de groun' des ez gayly ez
a June cricket. Ole Brer Tarrypin, he lay low in de
swamp. He had a wife en th'ee chilluns, ole Brer
Tarrypin did, en dey wuz all de ve'y spit en image er de
ole man. Ennybody w'at know one fum de udder gotter
take a spy-glass, en den dey er li'ble fer ter git fooled.

"Dat's de way marters stan' twel de day er de

race, en on dat day, ole Brer Tarrypin, en his ole
'oman, en his th'ee chilluns, dey got up 'fo' sun-up, en
went ter de place. De ole 'oman, she tuck 'er stan'
nigh de fus' mile-pos', she did, en de chilluns nigh de
udders, up ter de las', en dar old Brer Tarrypin, he
tuck his stan'. Bimeby, here come de fokes : Jedge
Buzzard, he come, en Miss Meadows en de gals, dey
come, en den yer come Brer Rabbit wid ribbins tied
'roun' his neck en streamin' fum his years. De fokes
all went ter de udder een' er de track fer ter see how
dey come out. W'en de time come Jedge Buzzard
strut 'roun' en pull out his watch, en holler out :

"'Gents, is you ready ?'

"Brer Rabbit, he say 'yes,' en ole Miss
Tarrypin holler 'go' fum de aidge er de
woods. Brer Rabbit, he lit out on de
race, en ole Miss Tarrypin, she put out
for home. Jedge
Buzzard, he riz
en skimmed
'long fer ter
see dat de race
wuz runned
fa'r. W'en Brer
Rabbit got ter

de fus mile-pos' wunner de Tarrypin chilluns crawl out
de woods, he did, en make fer de place. Berr Rabbit,
he holler out :

" ' Whar is you, Brer Tarrypin ? '

" ' Yer I come a bulgin',' sez de Tarrypin, sezee.

" Brer Rabbit so glad he's ahead dat he put out harder dan ever, en de Tarrypin, he make fer home. W'en he come ter de nex' pos', nudder Tarrypin crawl out er de woods.

" ' Whar is you, Brer Tarrypin ? ' sez Brer Rabbit, sezee.

" ' Yer I come a bilin',' sez de Tarrypin, sezee.

" Brer Rabbit, he lit out, he did, en come ter nex' pos', en dar wuz de Tarrypin. Den he come ter nex', en dar wuz de Tarrypin. Den he had one mo' mile fer ter run, en he feel like he gittin' bel-lust. Bimeby, ole Brer Tarrypin look way off down de road en he see Jedge Buz-zard sailin' 'long en he know hit's time fer 'im fer ter be up. So he scramble outen de woods, en roll 'cross de ditch, en shuffle thoo de crowd er folks en git ter de mile-pos' en crawl behime it. Bimeby, fus' news you know, yer come Brer Rabbit. He look 'roun' en

he don't see Brer Tarrypin, en den he squall
out :

"'Gimme de money, Brer Buzzard! Gimme de
money!'

"Den Miss Meadows en de gals, dey holler and laff
fit ter kill deyse'f, en ole Brer Tarrypin, he raise up
fum behime de pos' en sez, sezee :

"'Ef you'll gimme time fer ter ketch my breff,
gents en ladies, one en all, I speck I'll finger dat
money myse'f,' sezee, en sho nuff, Brer Tarrypin tie
de pu's 'roun' his neck en skaddle * off home."

"But, Uncle Remus," said the little boy, dolefully,
"that was cheating."

"Co'se, honey. De creeturs 'gun ter cheat, en
den fokes tuck it up, en hit keep on spreadin'. Hit
mighty ketchin', en you mine yo' eye, honey, dat somebody don't cheat you 'fo' yo' ha'r git gray ez de ole
nigger's."

---

* It may be interesting to note here that in all probability the
word "skedaddle," about which there was some controversy during
the war, came from the Virginia negro's use of "skaddle," which is
a corruption of "scatter." The matter, however, is hardly worth
referring to.

XIX.

THE FATE OF MR. JACK SPARROW.

" You'll tromple on dat bark twel hit won't be fitten fer ter fling 'way, let 'lone make hoss-collars out'n," said Uncle Remus, as the little boy came running into his cabin out of the rain. All over the floor long strips of " wahoo " bark were spread, and these the old man was weaving into horse-collars.

" I'll sit down, Uncle Remus," said the little boy.

" Well, den, you better, honey," responded the old man, " kaze I 'spizes fer ter have my wahoo trompled on. Ef 'twuz shucks, now, hit mout be diffunt, but I'm a gittin' too ole fer ter be projickin' longer shuck collars."

For a few minutes the old man went on with his work, but with a solemn air altogether unusual. Once or twice he sighed deeply, and the sighs ended in a prolonged groan, that seemed to the little boy to be the result of the most unspeakable mental agony. He knew by experience that he had done something which failed to meet the approval of Uncle Remus, and he tried to remember what it was, so as to frame an excuse; but his memory failed him. He could think of nothing he had done calculated to stir Uncle Remus's grief. He was not exactly seized with remorse, but he was very uneasy. Presently Uncle Remus looked at him in a sad and hopeless way, and asked :

" W'at dat long rigmarole you bin tellin' Miss
Sally 'bout yo' little brer dis mawnin ? "

" Which, Uncle Remus ? " asked the little boy,
blushing guiltily.

" Dat des w'at I'm a axin' un you now. I hear
Miss Sally say she's a gwineter stripe his jacket, en
den I knowed you bin tellin' on 'im."

" Well, Uncle Remus, he was pulling up your
onions, and then he went and flung a rock at me,"
said the child, plaintively.

" Lemme tell you dis," said the old man, laying
down the section of horse-collar he had been plaiting,
and looking hard at the little boy—" lemme tell you
dis—der ain't no way fer ter make tattlers en tail-
b'arers turn out good. No, dey ain't. I bin mixin'
up wid fokes now gwine on eighty year, en I ain't
seed no tattler come ter no good een'. Dat I ain't.
En ef ole man M'thoozlum wuz livin' clean twel yit,
he'd up'n tell you de same. Sho ez youer settin' dar.
You 'member w'at 'come er de bird w'at went tattlin'
'roun' 'bout Brer Rabbit ? "

The little boy didn't remember, but he was very
anxious to know, and he also wanted to know what
kind of a bird it was that so disgraced itself.

" Hit wuz wunner dese yer uppity little Jack
Sparrers, I speck," said the old man ; " dey wuz allers
bodder'n' longer udder fokes's bizness, en dey keeps at
it down ter dis day—peckin' yer, en pickin' dar, en

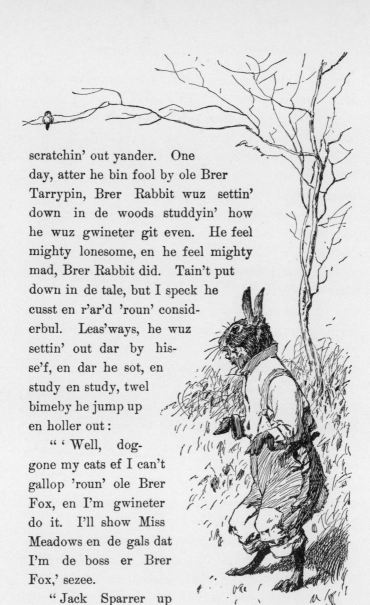

scratchin' out yander. One
day, atter he bin fool by ole Brer
Tarrypin, Brer Rabbit wuz settin'
down in de woods studdyin' how
he wuz gwineter git even. He feel
mighty lonesome, en he feel mighty
mad, Brer Rabbit did. Tain't put
down in de tale, but I speck he
cusst en r'ar'd 'roun' consid-
erbul. Leas'ways, he wuz
settin' out dar by his-
se'f, en dar he sot, en
study en study, twel
bimeby he jump up
en holler out :

" ' Well, dog-
gone my cats ef I can't
gallop 'roun' ole Brer
Fox, en I'm gwineter
do it. I'll show Miss
Meadows en de gals dat
I'm de boss er Brer
Fox,' sezee.

" Jack Sparrer up

in de tree, he hear Brer Rabbit, he did, en he sing
out :

"'I'm gwine tell Brer Fox! I'm gwine tell Brer
Fox! Chick-a-biddy-win'-a-blowin'-acuns-fallin'! I'm
gwine tell Brer Fox!'"

Uncle Remus accompanied the speech of the bird
with a peculiar whistling sound in his throat, that was
a marvelous imitation of a sparrow's chirp, and the
little boy clapped his hands with delight, and insisted
on a repetition.

"Dis kinder tarrify Brer Rabbit, en he skasely
know w'at he gwine do; but bimeby he study ter
hisse'f dat de man w'at see Brer Fox fus wuz boun'
ter have de inturn, en den he go hoppin' off to'rds
home. He didn't got fur w'en who should he meet
but Brer Fox, en den Brer Rabbit, he open up :

"'W'at dis twix' you en me, Brer Fox?' sez Brer
Rabbit, sezee. 'I hear tell you gwine ter sen' me ter
'struckshun, en nab my fambly, en 'stroy my shanty,'
sezee.

"Den Brer Fox he git mighty mad.

"'Who bin tellin' you all dis?' sezee.

"Brer Rabbit make like he didn't want ter tell, but
Brer Fox he 'sist en 'sist, twel at las' Brer Rabbit he
up en tell Brer Fox dat he hear Jack Sparrer say
all dis.

"'Co'se,' sez Brer Rabbit, sezee, 'w'en Brer Jack
Sparrer tell me dat I flew up, I did, en I use some

langwidge w'ich I'm mighty glad dey wern't no ladies 'roun' nowhars so dey could hear me go on,' sezee.

" Brer Fox he sorter gap, he did, en say he speck he better be sa'nter'n on.   But, bless yo' soul, honey, Brer Fox ain't sa'nter fur, 'fo' Jack Sparrer flipp down on a 'simmon-bush by de side er de road, en holler out :

" ' Brer Fox!   Oh, Brer Fox !—Brer Fox ! '

" Brer Fox he des sorter canter 'long, he did, en make like he don't hear 'im.   Den Jack Sparrer up'n sing out agin :

" ' Brer Fox!   Oh, Brer Fox !   Hole on, Brer Fox !   I got some news fer you.   Wait Brer Fox ! Hit'll 'stonish you.'

" Brer Fox he make like he don't see Jack Sparrer, ner needer do he hear 'im, but bimeby he lay down by de road, en sorter stretch hisse'f like he fixin' fer ter nap.   De tattlin' Jack Sparrer he flew'd 'long, en keep on callin' Brer Fox, but Brer Fox, he ain't sayin' nuthin'.   Den little Jack Sparrer, he hop down on de groun' en flutter 'roun' 'mongst de trash.   Dis

sorter 'track Brer Fox 'tenshun, en he look at de tattlin' bird, en de bird he keep on callin' :

"' I got sump'n fer ter tell you, Brer Fox.'

"' Git on my tail, little Jack Sparrer,' sez Brer Fox, sezee, ' kaze I'm de'f in one year, en I can't hear out'n de udder. Git on my tail,' sezee.

" Den de little bird he up'n hop on Brer Fox's tail.

"' Git on my back, little Jack Sparrer, kaze I'm de'f in one year en I can't hear out'n de udder.'

" Den de little bird hop on his back.

"' Hop on my head, little Jack Sparrer, kaze I'm de'f in bofe years.'

" Up hop de little bird.

"' Hop on my toof, little Jack Sparrer, kaze I'm de'f in one year en I can't hear out'n de udder.'

" De tattlin' little bird hop on Brer Fox's toof, en den—"

Here Uncle Remus paused, opened wide his mouth and closed it again in a way that told the whole story. *

---

* An Atlanta friend heard this story in Florida, but an alligator was substituted for the fox, and a little boy for the rabbit. There is another version in which the impertinent gosling goes to tell the fox something her mother has said, and is caught; and there may be other versions. I have adhered to the middle Georgia version, which is characteristic enough. It may be well to state that there are different versions of all the stories—the shrewd narrators of the mythology of the old plantation adapting themselves with ready tact to the years, tastes, and expectations of their juvenile audiences.

"Did the Fox eat the bird all—all—up?" asked the little boy.

"Jedge B'ar come 'long nex' day," replied Uncle Remus, "en he fine some fedders, en fum dat word went roun' dat ole man Squinch Owl done kotch nudder watzizname."

XX.

HOW MR. RABBIT SAVED HIS MEAT.

"One time," said Uncle Remus, whetting his knife slowly and thoughtfully on the palm of his hand, and gazing reflectively in the fire—"one time Brer Wolf—"

"Why, Uncle Remus!" the little boy broke in, "I thought you said the Rabbit scalded the Wolf to death a long time ago."

The old man was fairly caught and he knew it; but this made little difference to him. A frown gathered on his usually serene brow as he turned his gaze upon the child—a frown in which both scorn and indignation were visible. Then all at once he seemed to regain control of himself. The frown was chased away by a look of Christian resignation.

"Dar now! W'at I tell you?" he exclaimed as if addressing a witness concealed under the bed. "Ain't I done tole you so? Bless grashus! ef chilluns ain't gittin' so dey knows mo'n ole fokes, en dey'll

spute longer you en spute longer you, ceppin der ma
call um, w'ich I speck twon't be long 'fo' she will, en
den I'll set yere by de chimbly-cornder en git some
peace er mine.   W'en ole Miss wuz livin'," continued
the old man, still addressing some imaginary person,
" hit 'uz mo'n enny her chilluns 'ud dast ter do ter
come 'sputin' longer me, en Mars John'll tell you de
same enny day you ax 'im."

" Well, Uncle Remus, you know you said the
Rabbit poured hot water on the Wolf and killed him,"
said the little boy.

The old man pretended not to hear. He was engaged in searching among some scraps of leather under
his chair, and kept on talking to the imaginary person.
Finally, he found and drew forth a nicely plaited
whip-thong with a red snapper all waxed and knotted.

" I wuz fixin' up a w'ip fer a little chap," he continued, with a sigh, " but, bless grashus ! 'fo' I kin git
'er done, de little chap done grow'd up twel he know
mo'n I duz."

The child's eyes filled with tears and his lips began
to quiver, but he said nothing; whereupon Uncle
Remus immediately melted.

" I 'clar' to goodness," he said, reaching out and
taking the little boy tenderly by the hand, " ef you
ain't de ve'y spit en image er ole Miss w'en I brung
'er de las' news er de war. Hit's des like skeerin' up
a ghos' w'at you ain't fear'd un."

Then there was a pause, the old man patting the little child's hand caressingly.

" You ain't mad, is you, honey?" Uncle Remus asked finally, " kaze ef you is, I'm gwine out yere en butt my head 'gin de do' jam'."

But the little boy wasn't mad. Uncle Remus had conquered him and he had conquered Uncle Remus in pretty much the same way before. But it was some time before Uncle Remus would go on with the story. He had to be coaxed. At last, however, he settled himself back in the chair and began :

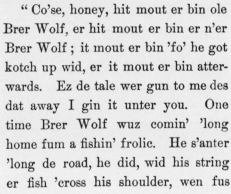

" Co'se, honey, hit mout er bin ole Brer Wolf, er hit mout er bin er n'er Brer Wolf ; it mout er bin 'fo' he got kotch up wid, er it mout er bin atterwards. Ez de tale wer gun to me des dat away I gin it unter you. One time Brer Wolf wuz comin' 'long home fum a fishin' frolic. He s'anter 'long de road, he did, wid his string er fish 'cross his shoulder, wen fus news you know ole Miss Pa'tridge, she hop outer de bushes en flutter 'long right at Brer Wolf nose. Brer Wolf he say ter hisse'f dat ole Miss

Pa'tridge tryin' fer ter toll 'im 'way fum her nes', en wid dat he lay his fish down en put out inter de bushes whar ole Miss Pa'tridge come fum, en 'bout dat time Brer Rabbit, he happen 'long. Dar wuz de fishes, en dar wuz Brer Rabbit, en w'en dat de case w'at you speck a sorter innerpen'ent man like Brer Rabbit gwine do? I kin tell you dis, dat dem fishes ain't stay whar Brer Wolf put um at, en w'en Brer Wolf come back dey wuz gone.

"Brer Wolf, he sot down en scratch his head, he did, en study en study, en den hit sorter rush inter his mine dat Brer Rabbit bin 'long dar, en den Brer Wolf, he put out fer Brer Rabbit house, en w'en he git dar he hail 'im. Brer Rabbit, he dunno nuthin' tall 'bout no fishes. Brer Wolf he up'n say he bleedzd ter b'leeve Brer Rabbit got dem fishes. Brer Rabbit 'ny it up en down, but Brer Wolf stan' to it dat Brer Rabbit got dem fishes. Brer Rabbit, he say dat if Brer Wolf b'leeve he got de fishes, den he give Brer Wolf lief fer ter kill de bes' cow he got. Brer Wolf, he tuck Brer Rabbit at his word, en go off ter de pastur' en drive up de cattle en kill Brer Rabbit bes' cow.

"Brer Rabbit, he hate mighty bad fer ter lose his cow, but he lay his plans, en he tell his chilluns dat he gwineter have dat beef yit. Brer Wolf, he bin tuck up by de patter-rollers 'fo' now, en he mighty skeerd un um, en fus news you know, yer come Brer

Rabbit hollerin' en tellin' Brer Wolf dat de patter-rollers comin'.

"'You run en hide, Brer Wolf,' sez Brer Rabbit, sezee, 'en I'll stay yer en take keer er de cow twel you gits back,' sezee.

"Soon's Brer Wolf hear talk er de patter-rollers, he scramble off inter de underbresh like he bin shot out'n a gun. En he want mo'n gone 'fo' Brer Rabbit, he whirl in en skunt de cow en salt de hide down, en den he tuck'n cut up de kyarkiss en stow it 'way in de smoke-'ouse, en den he tuck'n stick de een' er de cow-tail in de groun'. Atter he gone en done all dis, den Brer Rabbit he squall out fer Brer Wolf:

"'Run yer, Brer Wolf! Run yer! Yo' cow gwine in de groun'! Run yer!'

"W'en ole Brer Wolf got dar, w'ich he come er scootin', dar wuz Brer Rabbit hol'in' on ter de cow-tail, fer ter keep it fum gwine in de groun'. Brer Wolf, he kotch holt, en dey 'gin a pull er two en up come de tail. Den Brer Rabbit, he wink his off eye en say, sezee:

"'Dar! de tail done pull out en de cow gone,' sezee.

"But Brer Wolf he wer'n't de man fer ter give it up dat away, en he got 'im a spade, en a pick-axe, en a shovel, en he dig en dig fer dat cow twel diggin' wuz pas' all endu'unce, en ole Brer Rabbit he sot up dar in his front po'ch en smoke his seegyar. Eve'y time ole

Brer Wolf stuck de pick-axe in de clay, Brer Rabbit,
he giggle ter his chilluns:

"'He diggy, diggy, diggy, but no meat dar! He
diggy, diggy, diggy, but no meat dar!'

"Kase all de time de cow wuz layin' pile up in his
smoke-'ouse, en him en his chilluns wuz eatin' fried
beef en inguns eve'y time dey mouf water.

"Now den, honey, you take dis yer w'ip," continued the old man, twining the leather thong around
the little boy's neck, "en scamper up ter de big 'ouse
en tell Miss Sally fer ter gin you some un it de nex'
time she fine yo' tracks in de sugar-bairl."

XXI.

MR. RABBIT MEETS HIS MATCH AGAIN.

"DERE wuz nudder man dat sorter play it sharp on
Brer Rabbit," said Uncle Remus, as, by some mysterious process, he twisted a hog's bristle into the end of
a piece of thread—an operation which the little boy
watched with great interest. "In dem days," continued the old man, "de creeturs kyar'd on marters
same ez fokes. Dey went inter fahmin', en I speck ef
de troof wuz ter come out, dey kep' sto', en had der
camp-meetin' times en der bobbycues w'en de wedder
wuz 'greeble."

Uncle Remus evidently thought that the little boy

wouldn't like to hear of any further discomfiture of
Brer Rabbit, who had come to be a sort of hero, and
he was not mistaken.

"I thought the Terrapin was the only one that
fooled the Rabbit," said the little boy, dismally.

"Hit's des like I tell you, honey. Dey ain't no
smart man, 'cep' w'at dey's a smarter. Ef ole Brer
Rabbit hadn't er got kotch up wid, de nabers 'ud er
took 'im for a h'ant, en in dem times dey bu'nt
witches 'fo' you could squinch yo' eyeballs. Dey did
dat."

"Who fooled the Rabbit this time?" the little boy
asked.

When Uncle Remus had the bristle "sot" in the
thread, he proceeded with the story:

"One time Brer Rabbit en ole Brer Buzzard
'cluded dey'd sorter go snacks, en crap tergedder. Hit
wuz a mighty good year, en de truck tu'n out monstus
well, but bimeby, w'en de time come fer dividjun, hit
come ter light dat ole Brer Buzzard ain't got nuthin'.
De crap wuz all gone, en dey want nuthin' dar fer ter
show fer it. Brer Rabbit, he make like he in a wuss
fix'n Brer Buzzard, en he mope 'roun', he did, like he
fear'd dey gwineter sell 'im out.

"Brer Buzzard, he ain't sayin' nuthin', but he keep
up a monstus thinkin', en one day he come 'long en
holler en tell Brer Rabbit dat he done fine rich gole-
mine des 'cross de river.

" ' You come en go 'longer me, Brer Rabbit,' sez Brer Tukky Buzzard, sezee. ' I'll scratch en you kin grabble, en 'tween de two un us   we'll make short wuk er dat gole-mine,'   sezee.

" Brer Rabbit, he wuz high up fer de job, but he study en study, he did, how he gwineter git 'cross de water, kaze ev'y time he git his foot wet all de fambly kotch cole. Den he up'n ax Brer Buzzard how he gwine do, en Brer Buzzard he up'n say dat he kyar Brer Rabbit 'cross, en wid dat ole Brer Buzzard, he squot down, he did, en spread his wings, en Brer Rabbit, he mounted, en up dey riz." There was pause.

" What did the Buzzard do then ? " asked the little boy.

" Dey riz," continued Uncle Remus, " en w'en dey lit, dey lit in de top er de highest sorter pine, en de pine w'at dey lit in wuz growin' on er ilun, en de ilun wuz in de middle er de river, wid de deep water runnin' all 'roun'. Dey ain't mo'n lit 'fo' Brer Rabbit, he know w'ich way de win' 'uz blowin', en by de time ole Brer Buzzard got hisse'f ballunce on a lim', Brer Rabbit, he up'n say, sezee:

"'W'iles we er res'n here, Brer Buzzard, en bein's you bin so good, I got sump'n fer ter tell you,' sezee. 'I got a gole-mine er my own, one w'at I make my-se'f, en I speck we better go back ter mine 'fo' we bodder 'longer yone,' sezee.

"Den ole Brer Buzzard, he laff, he did, twel he shake, en Brer Rabbit, he sing out:

"'Hole on, Brer Buzzard! Don't flop yo' wings w'en you laff, kaze den ef you duz, sump'n 'ill drap fum up yer, en my gole-mine won't do you no good, en needer will yone do me no good.'

"But 'fo' dey got down fum dar, Brer Rabbit done tole all 'bout de crap, en he hatter promus fer ter 'vide fa'r en squar. So Brer Buzzard, he kyar 'im back, en Brer Rabbit he walk weak in de knees a mont' atterwuds."

XXII.

A STORY ABOUT THE LITTLE RABBITS.

"Fine um whar you will en w'en you may," remarked Uncle Remus with emphasis, "good chilluns
allers gits tuck keer on.   Dar wuz Brer Rabbit's
chilluns ; dey minded der daddy en mammy fum day's
een' ter day's een'.   W'en ole man Rabbit say ' scoot,'
dey scooted, en w'en ole Miss Rabbit say ' scat,' dey
scatted.   Dey did dat.   En dey kep der cloze clean,
en dey ain't had no smut on der nose nudder."

Involuntarily the hand of the little boy went up to
his face, and he scrubbed the end of his nose with his
coat-sleeve.

"Dey wuz good chilluns," continued the old man,
heartily, "en ef dey hadn't er bin, der wuz one time
w'en dey wouldn't er bin no little rabbits—na'er one.
Dat's w'at."

"What time was that, Uncle Remus?" the little
boy asked.

"De time w'en Brer Fox drapt in at Brer Rabbit
house, en didn't foun' nobody dar ceppin' de little
Rabbits.   Ole Brer Rabbit, he wuz off some'rs raiding
on a collard patch, en ole Miss Rabbit she wuz tendin'
on a quiltin' in de naberhood, en wiles de little Rabbits
wuz playin' hidin'-switch, in drapt Brer Fox.   De little Rabbits wuz so fat dat dey fa'rly make his mouf

water, but he 'member 'bout Brer Wolf, en he skeered
fer ter gobble um up ceppin' he got some skuse. De

little Rabbits, dey
mighty skittish, en
dey sorter huddle
deyse'f up ter-
gedder en watch
Brer Fox mo-
tions.   Brer
Fox, he sot
dar en study
w'at sorter skuse he
gwineter make up.
Bimeby he see a great big
stalk er sugar-cane stan'in' up in de cornder, en he cle'r
up his th'oat en talk biggity :

"' Yer ! you young Rabs dar, sail 'roun' yer en
broke me a piece er dat sweetnin'-tree,' sezee, en den
he koff.

" De little Rabbits, dey got out de sugar-cane, dey
did, en dey rastle wid it, en sweat over it, but twan't
no use. Dey couldn't broke it. Brer Fox, he make
like he ain't watchin', but he keep on holler'n :

"' Hurry up dar, Rabs ! I'm a waitin' on you.'

" En de little Rabbits, dey hustle 'roun' en rastle
wid it, but dey couldn't broke it. Bimeby dey hear
little bird singin' on top er de house, en de song w'at
de little bird sing wuz dish yer :

> " ' Take yo' toofies en gnyaw it,
>   Take yo' toofies en saw it,
>   Saw it en yoke it,
>   En den you kin broke it.'

" Den de little Rabbits, dey git mighty glad, en
dey gnyawed de cane mos' 'fo' ole Brer Fox could git
his legs oncrosst, en w'en dey kyard 'im de cane, Brer
Fox, he sot dar en study how he gwineter make some
mo' skuse fer nabbin' un um, en bimeby he git up en
git down de sifter w'at wuz hangin' on de wall, en
holler out :

" ' Come yer, Rabs ! Take dish yer sifter, en run
down't de spring en fetch me some fresh water.'

" De little Rabbits, dey run down't de spring, en
try ter dip up de water wid de sifter, but co'se hit all
run out, en hit keep on runnin' out, twell bimeby de
little Rabbits sot down en 'gun ter cry.   Den de little
bird settin' up in de tree he begin fer ter sing, en dish
yer's de song w'at he sing :

> " ' Sifter hole water same ez a tray,
>   Ef you fill it wid moss en dob it wid clay ;
>   De Fox git madder de longer you stay—
>   Fill it wid moss en dob it wid clay.'

" Up dey jump, de little Rabbits did, en dey fix de
sifter so 'twon't leak, en den dey kyar de water ter ole
Brer Fox.   Den Brer Fox he git mighty mad, en
p'int out a great big stick er wood, en tell de little
Rabbits fer ter put dat on de fier.   De little chaps dey
got 'roun' de wood, dey did, en dey lif' at it so hard

twel dey could see der own sins, but de wood ain't budge. Den dey hear de little bird singin', en

dish yer's de song w'at he sing :

> " ' Spit in yo' han's en tug it en toll it,
> En git behine it, en push it, en pole it;
> Spit in yo' han's en r'ar back en roll it.'

" En des 'bout de time dey got de wood on de fier, der daddy, he come skippin' in, en de little bird, he flew'd away. Brer Fox, he seed his game wuz up, en 'twan't long 'fo' he make his skuse en start fer ter go.

" ' You better stay en take a snack wid me, Brer Fox,' sez Brer Rabbit, sezee. ' Sence Brer Wolf done quit comin' en settin' up wid me, I gittin' so I feels right lonesome dese long nights,' sezee.

" But Brer Fox, he button up his coat-collar tight en des put out fer home. En dat w'at you better do, honey, kaze I see Miss Sally's shadder sailin' backerds en for'ds 'fo' de winder, en de fus' news you know she'll be spectin' un you."

XXIII.

MR. RABBIT AND MR. BEAR.

" DAR wuz one season," said Uncle Remus, pulling
thoughtfully at his whiskers, " w'en Brer Fox say to
hisse'f dat he speck he better whirl in en plant a
goober-patch, en in dem days, mon, hit wuz tech en
go.   De wud wern't mo'n out'n his mouf 'fo' de
groun' 'uz brok'd up en de goobers 'uz planted.   Ole
Brer Rabbit, he sot off en watch de motions, he did,
en he sorter shet one eye en sing to his chilluns :

> " ' Ti-yi !   Tungalee ?
> I eat um pea, I pick um pea.
> Hit grow in de groun', hit grow so free ;
> Ti-yi ! dem goober pea.'

" Sho' 'nuff w'en de goobers 'gun ter ripen up,
eve'y time Brer Fox go down ter his patch, he fine
whar somebody bin grabblin' 'mongst de vines, en he
git mighty mad.   He sorter speck who de somebody
is, but ole Brer Rabbit he cover his tracks so cute dat
Brer Fox dunner how ter ketch 'im.   Bimeby, one
day Brer Fox take a walk all roun' de groun'-pea
patch, en 'twan't long 'fo' he fine a crack in de fence
whar de rail done bin rub right smoove, en right dar
he sot 'im a trap.   He tuck'n ben' down a hick'ry
saplin', growin' in de fence-cornder, en tie one een' un

a plow-line on de top, en in de udder een' he fix a
loop-knot, en dat he fasten wid a trigger right in de
crack.   Nex' mawnin' w'en ole Brer Rabbit come slippin' 'long   en crope thoo de crack, de loop-
knot kotch   'im behime de fo' legs, en de saplin' flew'd   up, en dar he wuz 'twix' de heavens
en de yeth.   Dar he swung, en he fear'd he
                   gwineter fall, en he fear'd
                   he wer'n't gwineter fall.

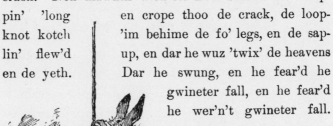

W'ile he wuz a fixin' up a
tale fer Brer Fox, he hear a
lumberin' down de road, en
present'y yer cum ole Brer B'ar
amblin' 'long fum whar he bin takin' a bee-tree.   Brer
Rabbit, he hail 'im :

"' Howdy, Brer B'ar ! '

"Brer B'ar, he look 'roun en bimeby he see Brer
Rabbit swingin' fum de saplin', en he holler out :

"'Heyo, Brer Rabbit! How you come on dis mawnin'?'

"'Much oblije, I'm middlin', Brer B'ar,' sez Brer Rabbit, sezee.

"Den Brer B'ar, he ax Brer Rabbit w'at he doin' up dar in de elements, en Brer Rabbit, he up'n say he makin' dollar minnit. Brer B'ar, he say how. Brer Rabbit say he keepin' crows out'n Brer Fox's groun'-pea patch, en den he ax Brer B'ar ef he don't wanter make dollar minnit, kaze he got big fambly er chilluns fer ter take keer un, en den he make sech nice skeer-crow. Brer B'ar 'low dat he take de job, en den Brer Rabbit show 'im how ter ben' down de saplin', en 'twan't long 'fo' Brer B'ar wuz swingin' up dar in Brer Rabbit place. Den Brer Rabbit, he put out fer Brer Fox house, en w'en he got dar he sing out:

"'Brer Fox! Oh, Brer Fox! Come out yer, Brer Fox, en I'll show you de man w'at bin stealin' yo' goobers.'

"Brer Fox, he grab up his walkin'-stick, en bofe un um went runnin' back down ter der goober-patch, en w'en dey got dar, sho 'nuff, dar wuz ole Brer B'ar.

"'Oh, yes! youer kotch, is you?' sez Brer Fox, en 'fo' Brer B'ar could 'splain, Brer Rabbit he jump up en down, en holler out:

"'Hit 'im in de mouf, Brer Fox; hit 'im in de mouf'; en Brer Fox, he draw back wid de walkin'-

cane, en blip he tuck 'im, en eve'y time Brer B'ar'd try
ter 'splain, Brer Fox'd shower down on him.

"W'iles all dis 'uz gwine on, Brer Rabbit, he slip
off en git in a mud-hole en des lef' his eyes stickin'
out, kaze he know'd dat Brer B'ar'd be a comin' atter

'im. Sho 'nuff, bimeby here come Brer B'ar down de
road, en w'en he git ter de mud-hole, he say :

"'Howdy, Brer Frog ; is you seed Brer Rabbit go
by yer ?'

"'He des gone by,' sez Brer Rabbit, en ole man

B'ar tuck off down de road like a skeer'd mule, en Brer Rabbit, he come out en dry hisse'f in de sun, en go home ter his fambly same ez enny udder man."

"The Bear didn't catch the Rabbit, then?" inquired the little boy, sleepily.

"Jump up fum dar, honey!" exclaimed Uncle Remus, by way of reply. "I ain't got no time fer ter be settin' yer proppin' yo' eyeleds open."

XXIV.

MR. BEAR CATCHES OLD MR. BULL-FROG.

"WELL, Uncle Remus," said the little boy, counting to see if he hadn't lost a marble somewhere, "the Bear didn't catch the Rabbit after all, did he?"

"Now you talkin', honey," replied the old man, his earnest face breaking up into little eddies of smiles —"now you talkin' sho. 'Tain't bin proned inter no Brer B'ar fer ter kotch Brer Rabbit. Hit sorter like settin' a mule fer ter trap a hummin'-bird. But Brer B'ar, he tuck'n got hisse'f inter some mo' trubble, w'ich it look like it mighty easy. Ef folks could make der livin' longer gittin' inter trubble," continued the old man, looking curiously at the little boy, "ole Miss Favers wouldn't be bodder'n yo' ma fer ter borry a cup full er sugar eve'y now en den; en it look like ter me dat I knows a nigger dat wouldn't be squattin' 'roun' yer makin' dese yer fish-baskits."

"How did the Bear get into more trouble, Uncle Remus?" asked the little boy.

"Natchul, honey.   Brer B'ar, he tuck a notion dat ole Brer Bull-frog wuz de man wa't fool 'im, en he say dat he'd come up wid 'im ef 'twuz a year atter-wuds.   But 'twan't no year, an 'twan't no mont', en mo'n dat, hit wan't skasely a week, w'en bimeby one day Brer B'ar wuz gwine home fum de takin' un a bee-tree, en lo en beholes, who should he see but ole Brer Bull-frog settin' out on de aidge er de mud - puddle fas' 'sleep! Brer B'ar drap his axe, he did, en crope up, en retch out wid his paw, en scoop ole Brer Bull-frog in des dis away." Here the old man used his hand ladle-fashion, by way of illustration.   "He scoop 'im in, en dar he wuz. W'en Brer B'ar got his clampers on 'im good, he sot down en talk at 'im.

"'Howdy, Brer Bull-frog, howdy! En how yo'

fambly? I hope deyer well, Brer Bull-frog, kaze dis day you got some bizness wid me w'at'll las' you a mighty long time.'

"Brer Bull-frog, he dunner w'at ter say. He dunner wat's up, en he don't say nuthin'. Ole Brer B'ar he keep runnin' on :

"'Youer de man w'at tuck en fool me 'bout Brer Rabbit t'er day. You had yo' fun, Brer Bull-frog, en now I'll git mine.'

"Den Brer Bull-frog, he gin ter git skeerd, he did, en he up'n say :

"'W'at I bin doin', Brer B'ar? How I bin foolin' you?'

"Den Brer B'ar laff, en make like he dunno, but he keep on talkin'.

"'Oh, no, Brer Bull-frog! You ain't de man w'at stick yo' head up out'n de water en tell me Brer Rabbit done gone on by. Oh, no! you ain't de man. I boun' you ain't. 'Bout dat time, you wuz at home with yo' fambly, whar you allers is. I dunner whar you wuz, but I knows whar you is, Brer Bull-frog, en hit's you en me fer it. Atter de sun goes down dis day you don't fool no mo' folks gwine 'long dis road.'

"Co'se, Brer Bull-frog dunner w'at Brer B'ar drivin' at, but he know sump'n hatter be done, en dat mighty soon, kaze Brer B'ar 'gun to snap his jaws ter-gedder en foam at de mouf, en Brer Bull-frog holler out :

" ' Oh, pray, Brer B'ar ! Lemme off dis time, en I
won't never do so no mo'. Oh, pray, Brer B'ar ! do
lemme off dis time, en I'll show you de fattes' bee-
tree in de woods.'

" Ole Brer B'ar, he chomp his toofies en foam at
de mouf. Brer Bull-frog he des up'n squall :

" ' Oh, pray, Brer B'ar ! I won't never do so no
mo' ! Oh, pray, Brer B'ar ! Lemme off dis time ! '

" But ole Brer B'ar say he gwineter make way wid
'im, en den he sot en study, ole Brer B'ar did, how he
gwineter squench Brer Bull-frog. He know he can't
drown 'im, en he ain't got no fier fer ter bu'n 'im, en
he git mighty pestered. Bimeby ole Brer Bull-frog,
he sorter stop his cryin' en his boo-hooin', en he up'n
say :

" ' Ef you gwineter kill me, Brer B'ar, kyar me ter
dat big flat rock out dar on de aidge er de mill-pon',
whar I kin see my fambly, en atter I see um, den you
kin take you axe en sqush me.'

" Dis look so fa'r and squar' dat Brer B'ar he 'gree,
en he take ole Brer Bull-frog by wunner his behime
legs, en sling his axe on his shoulder, en off he put fer
de big flat rock. When he git dar he lay Brer Bull-
frog down on de rock, en Brer Bull-frog make like he
lookin' 'roun' fer his folks. Den Brer B'ar, he draw
long breff en pick up his axe. Den he spit in his
han's en draw back en come down on de rock—
pow ! "

"Did he kill the Frog, Uncle Remus?" asked the
little boy, as the old man paused to scoop up a thimble-
ful of glowing embers in his pipe.

"'Deed, en dat he didn't, honey. 'Twix' de time
w'en Brer B'ar raise up wid his axe en w'en he come

down wid it, ole Brer Bull-frog he lipt up en dove
down in de mill-pon', kerblink-kerblunk! En w'en he
riz way out in de pon' he riz a singin', en dish yer's de
song w'at he sing:

> "'Ingle-go-jang, my joy, my joy—
> Ingle-go-jang, my joy!
> I'm right at home, my joy, my joy—
> Ingle-go-jang, my joy!'"

"That's a mighty funny song," said the little boy.

"Funny now, I speck," said the old man, "but
'twern't funny in dem days, en 'twouldn't be funny
now ef folks know'd much 'bout de Bull-frog langwidge ez dey useter. Dat's w'at."

XXV.

HOW MR. RABBIT LOST HIS FINE BUSHY TAIL.

" One time," said Uncle Remus, sighing heavily and settling himself back in his seat with an air of melancholy resignation—" one time Brer Rabbit wuz gwine 'long down de road shakin' his big bushy tail, en feelin' des ez scrumpshus ez a bee-martin wid a fresh bug." Here the old man paused and glanced at the little boy, but it was evident that the youngster had become so accustomed to the marvelous developments of Uncle Remus's stories, that the extraordinary statement made no unusual impression upon him. Therefore the old man began again, and this time in a louder and more insinuating tone :

" One time ole man Rabbit, he wuz gwine 'long down de road shakin' his long, bushy tail, en feelin' mighty biggity."

This was effective.

" Great goodness, Uncle Remus ! " exclaimed the little boy in open-eyed wonder, " everybody knows that rabbits haven't got long, bushy tails."

The old man shifted his position in his chair and allowed his venerable head to drop forward until his whole appearance was suggestive of the deepest dejection ; and this was intensified by a groan that seemed to be the result of great mental agony. Final-

ly he spoke, but not as addressing himself to the little
boy.

"I notices dat dem fokes w'at makes a great 'miration 'bout w'at dey knows is des de fokes w'ich you
can't put no 'pennunce in w'en de
'cashun come up. Yer one un um
now, en he done come en excuse me
er 'lowin' dat rabbits is
got long, bushy tails,
w'ich goodness knows
ef I'd a dremp' it, I'd
a whirl in en on dremp
it."

"Well, but Uncle Re-
mus, you said rabbits had
long, bushy tails," replied the
little boy. "Now you know
you did."

"Ef I ain't fergit it off'n
my mine, I say dat ole Brer
Rabbit wuz gwine down de big road shakin' his long,
bushy tail. Dat w'at I say, en dat I stan's by."

The little boy looked puzzled, but he didn't say
anything. After a while the old man continued:

"Now, den, ef dat's 'greed ter, I'm gwine on, en
ef tain't 'greed ter, den I'm gwineter pick up my cane
en look atter my own intrust. I got wuk lyin' roun'
yer dat's des natally gittin' moldy."

The little boy still remained quiet, and Uncle Remus proceeded :

" One day Brer Rabbit wuz gwine down de road
shakin' his long, bushy tail,
w'en who should he strike up
wid but ole Brer Fox gwine
amblin' long wid a big string
er fish ! W'en dey pass de
time er day wid
wunner   nudder,
Brer Rabbit, he
open up de con-
fab, he did,
en he ax
Brer Fox
whar he
git dat

nice string er fish, en
Brer Fox, he up'n 'spon'
dat he kotch um, en Brer Rabbit, he say whar'bouts,

en Brer Fox, he say down at de babtizin' creek, en
Brer Rabbit he ax how, kaze in dem days dey wuz
monstus fon' er minners, en Brer Fox, he sot down
on a log, he did, en he up'n tell Brer Rabbit dat all
he gotter do fer ter git er big mess er minners is
ter go ter de creek atter sun down, en drap his tail
in de water en set dar twel day-light, en den draw up
a whole armful er fishes, en dem w'at he don't want,
he kin fling back. Right dar's whar Brer Rabbit
drap his watermillion, kaze he tuck'n sot out dat
night en went a fishin'. De.wedder wuz sorter cole,
en Brer Rabbit, he got 'im a bottle er dram en put
out fer de creek, en w'en he git dar he pick out a
good place, en he sorter squot down, he did, en let
his tail hang in de water. He sot dar, en he sot dar,
en he drunk his dram, en he think he gwineter freeze,
but bimeby day come, en dar he wuz. He make a
pull, en he feel like he comin' in two, en he fetch
nudder jerk, en lo en beholes, whar wuz his tail ? "

There was a long pause.

" Did it come off, Uncle Remus ? " asked the little
boy, presently.

" She did dat ! " replied the old man with unction.
" She did dat, and dat w'at make all deze yer bob-tail
rabbits w'at you see hoppin' en skaddlin' thoo de
woods."

" Are they all that way just because the old Rabbit
lost his tail in the creek ? " asked the little boy.

"Dat's it, honey," replied the old man. "Dat's w'at dey tells me. Look like dey er bleedzd ter take atter der pa."

XXVI.

MR. TERRAPIN SHOWS HIS STRENGTH.

"Brer Tarrypin wuz de out'nes' man," said Uncle Remus, rubbing his hands together contemplatively, and chuckling to himself in a very significant manner ; "he wuz de out'nes' man er de whole gang. He wuz dat."

The little boy sat perfectly quiet, betraying no impatience when Uncle Remus paused to hunt, first in one pocket and then in another, for enough crumbs of tobacco to replenish his pipe. Presently the old man proceeded :

"One night Miss Meadows en de gals dey gun a candy-pullin', en so many er de nabers come in 'sponse ter de invite dat dey hatter put de 'lasses in de wash pot en b'il' de fier in de yard. Brer B'ar, he hope * Miss Meadows bring de wood, Brer Fox, he men' de fier, Brer Wolf, he kep' de dogs off, Brer Rabbit, he grease de bottom er de plates fer ter keep de candy fum stickin', en Brer Tarrypin, he klum up in a cheer,

* Holp; helped.

en say he'd watch en see dat de 'lasses didn't bile over.   Dey wuz all dere, en dey wern't cuttin' up no didos, nudder, kaze Miss Meadows, she done put her foot down, she did, en say dat w'en dey come ter her place dey hatter hang up a flag er truce at de front gate en 'bide by it.

"Well, den, w'iles dey wuz all a settin' dar en de 'lasses wuz a bilin' en a blubberin', dey got ter runnin' on talkin' mighty biggity.   Brer Rabbit, he say he de swiffes'; but Brer Tarrypin, he rock 'long in de cheer en watch de 'lasses.   Brer Fox, he say he

de sharpes', but Brer Tarrypin he rock 'long.   Brer Wolf, de say he de mos' suvvigus, but Brer Tarrypin,

he rock en he rock 'long. Brer B'ar, he say he de
mos' stronges', but Brer Tarrypin he rock, en he keep
on rockin'. Bimeby he sorter shet one eye, en say,
sezee :

" ' Hit look like 'periently dat de ole hardshell ain't
nowhars 'longside er dis crowd, yit yer I is, en I'm de
same man w'at show Brer Rabbit dat he ain't de
swiffes' ; en I'm de same man w'at kin show Brer B'ar
dat he ain't de stronges',' sezee.

" Den dey all laff en holler, kaze it look like Brer
B'ar mo' stronger dan a steer. Bimeby, Miss Meadows, she up'n ax, she did, how he gwine do it.

" ' Gimme a good strong rope,' sez Brer Tarrypin,
sezee, ' en lemme git in er puddle er water, en den let
Brer B'ar see ef he kin pull me out,' sezee.

" Den dey all laff g'in, en Brer B'ar, he ups en sez,
sezee : ' We ain't got no rope,' sezee.

" ' No,' sez Brer Tarrypin, sezee, ' en needer is you
got de strenk,' sezee, en den Brer Tarrypin, he rock en
rock 'long, en watch de 'lasses a bilin' en a blubberin'.

" Atter w'ile Miss Meadows, she up en say, she did,
dat she'd take'n loan de young men her bed-cord, en
w'iles de candy wuz a coolin' in de plates, dey could all
go ter de branch en see Brer Tarrypin kyar out his
projick. Brer Tarrypin," continued Uncle Remus, in
a tone at once confidential and argumentative, " wern't
much bigger'n de pa'm er my han', en it look mighty
funny fer ter year 'im braggin' 'bout how he kin out-

pull Brer B'ar. But dey got de bed-cord atter w'ile, en den dey all put out ter de branch. W'en Brer Tarrypin fine de place he wanter, he tuck one een' er de bed-cord, en gun de yuther een' to Brer B'ar.

" ' Now den, ladies en gents,' sez Brer Tarrypin, sezee, ' you all go wid Brer B'ar up dar in de woods en I'll stay yer, en w'en you year me holler, den's de time fer Brer B'ar fer ter see ef he kin haul in de slack er de rope. You all take keer er dat ar een',' sezee, ' en I'll take keer er dish yer een',' sezee.

" Den dey all put out en lef' Brer Tarrypin at de branch, en w'en dey got good en gone, he dove down

inter de water, he did, en tie de bedcord hard en fas'
ter wunner deze yer big clay-roots, en den he riz up en
gin a whoop.

"Brer B'ar he wrop de bed-cord roun' his han', en
wink at de gals, en wid dat he gin a big juk, but Brer
Tarrypin ain't budge. Den he take bofe han's en gin
a big pull, but, all de same, Brer Tarrypin ain't budge.
Den he tu'n 'roun', he did, en put de rope cross his
shoulders en try ter walk off wid Brer Tarrypin, but
Brer Tarrypin look like he don't feel like walkin'.
Den Brer Wolf he put in en hope Brer B'ar pull, but
des like he didn't, en den dey all hope 'im, en, bless
grashus! w'iles dey wuz all a pullin', Brer Tarrypin,
he holler, en ax um w'y dey don't take up de slack.
Den w'en Brer Tarrypin feel um quit pullin', he dove
down, he did, en ontie de rope, en by de time dey got
ter de branch, Brer Tarrypin, he wuz settin' in de
aidge er de water des ez natchul ez de nex' un, en he
up'n say, sezee :

"'Dat las' pull er yone wuz a mighty stiff un, en a
leetle mo'n you'd er had me,' sezee. 'Youer monstus
stout, Brer B'ar,' sezee, 'en you pulls like a yoke er
steers, but I sorter had de purchis on you,' sezee.

"Den Brer B'ar, bein's his mouf 'gun ter water
atter de sweetnin', he up'n say he speck de candy's
ripe, en off dey put atter it!"

"It's a wonder," said the little boy, after a while,
"that the rope didn't break."

"Break who?" exclaimed Uncle Remus, with a touch of indignation in his tone—"break who? In dem days, Miss Meadows's bed-cord would a hilt a mule."

This put an end to whatever doubts the child might have entertained.

XXVII.

WHY MR. POSSUM HAS NO HAIR ON HIS TAIL.

"Hit look like ter me," said Uncle Remus, frowning, as the little boy came hopping and skipping into the old man's cabin, "dat I see a young un 'bout yo' size playin' en makin' free wid dem ar chilluns er ole Miss Favers's yistiddy, en w'en I seed dat, I drap my axe, en I come in yer en sot flat down right whar youer settin' now, en I say ter myse'f dat it's 'bout time fer ole Remus fer ter hang up en quit. Dat's des zackly w'at I say."

"Well, Uncle Remus, they called me," said the little boy, in a penitent tone. "They come and called me, and said they had a pistol and some powder over there."

"Dar now!" exclaimed the old man, indignantly. "Dar now! w'at I bin sayin'? Hit's des a born blessin' dat you wa'n't brung home on a litter wid bofe eyeballs hangin' out en one year clean gone; dat's w'at 'tis! Hit's des a born blessin'. Hit hope me up might'ly de udder day w'en I hear Miss Sally layin' down de law 'bout you en dem Favers chillun, yit, lo en beholes, de fus news I knows yer you is han'-in-glove wid um. Hit's nuff fer ter fetch ole Miss right up out'n dat berryin'-groun' fum down dar in Putmon County, en w'at yo' gram'ma wouldn't er stood me en yo' ma ain't gwineter stan' nudder, en de nex' time I hear 'bout sech a come off ez dis, right den en dar I'm boun' ter lay de case 'fo' Miss Sally. Dem Favers's wa'n't no 'count 'fo' de war, en dey wa'n't no 'count endurin' er de war, en dey ain't no 'count atterwards, en w'iles my head's hot you ain't gwineter go mixin' up yo'se'f wid de riff-raff er creashun."

The little boy made no further attempt to justify his conduct. He was a very wise little boy, and he knew that, in Uncle Remus's eyes, he had been guilty of a flagrant violation of the family code. Therefore, instead of attempting to justify himself, he pleaded guilty, and promised that he would never do so any more. After this there was a long period of silence, broken only by the vigorous style in which Uncle Remus puffed away at his pipe. This was the invariable result. Whenever the old man had occasion to reprimand the little boy—and the occasions were frequent —he would relapse into a dignified but stubborn silence. Presently the youngster drew forth from his pocket a long piece of candle. The sharp eyes of the old man saw it at once.

"Don't you come a tellin' me dat Miss Sally gun you dat," he exclaimed, "kaze she didn't. En I lay you hatter be monstus sly 'fo' you gotter chance fer ter snatch up dat piece er cannle."

"Well, Uncle Remus," the little boy explained, "it was lying there all by itself, and I just thought I'd fetch it out to you."

"Dat's so, honey," said Uncle Remus, greatly mollified ; " dat's so, kaze by now some er dem yuther niggers 'ud er done had her lit up. Dey er mighty biggity, dem house niggers is, but I notices dat dey don't let nuthin' pass. Dey goes 'long wid der han's en der mouf open, en w'at one don't ketch de tother one do."

There was another pause, and finally the little boy said :

"Uncle Remus, you know you promised to-day to tell me why the 'Possum has no hair on his tail."

"Law, honey ! ain't you done gone en fergot dat off'n yo' mine yit ? Hit look like ter me," continued the old man, leisurely refilling his pipe, " dat she sorter run like dis : One time ole Brer Possum, he git so hungry, he did, dat he bleedzd fer ter have a mess er 'simmons. He monstus lazy man, old Brer Possum wuz, but bimeby his stummuck 'gun ter growl en holler at 'im so dat he des hatter rack 'roun' en hunt

up sump'n ; en w'iles he wuz rackin' 'roun', who sh'd
he run up wid but Brer Rabbit, en dey wuz hail-
fellers, kaze Brer Possum, he ain't bin bodder'n Brer
Rabbit like dem yuther creeturs.   Dey sot down by de
side er de big road, en dar dey
jabber en confab 'mong wunner
nudder, twel bimeby old Brer
Possum, he take 'n tell
Brer Rabbit dat he mos'

pe'sh out, en Brer
Rabbit, he lip up
in de a'r, he did, en
smack his han's tergedder, en say dat he know right
whar Brer Possum kin git a bait er 'simmons.   Den
Brer Possum, he say whar, en Brer Rabbit, he say
w'ich 'twuz over at Brer B'ar's 'simmon orchard."

   " Did the Bear have a 'simmon orchard, Uncle Remus ? " the little boy asked.

   " Co'se, honey, kaze in dem days Brer B'ar wuz a

bee-hunter. He make his livin' findin' bee trees, en de
way he fine um he plant 'im some 'simmon-trees, w'ich
de bees dey'd come ter suck de 'simmons en den ole
Brer B'ar he'd watch um whar dey'd go, en den he'd
be mighty ap' fer ter come up wid um. No matter
'bout dat, de 'simmon patch 'uz dar des like I tell you,
en ole Brer Possum mouf 'gun ter water soon's he
year talk un um, en mos' 'fo' Brer Rabbit done tellin'
'im de news, Brer Possum, he put out, he did, en
'twa'n't long 'fo' he wuz perch up in de highes' tree
in Brer B'ar 'simmon patch. But Brer Rabbit, he
done 'termin' fer ter see some fun, en w'iles all dis 'uz
gwine on, he run 'roun' ter Brer B'ar house, en holler
en tell 'im w'ich dey wuz somebody 'stroyin' un
his 'simmons, en Brer B'ar, he hustle off fer ter
ketch 'im.

"Eve'y now en den Brer Possum think he year
Brer B'ar comin', but he keep on sayin', sezee :

" ' I'll des git one 'simmon mo' en den I'll go ; one
'simmon mo' en den I'll go.'

" Las' he year Brer B'ar comin' sho nuff, but 'twuz
de same ole chune—' One 'simmon mo' en den I'll go '
—en des 'bout dat time Brer B'ar busted inter de patch,
en gin de tree a shake, en Brer Possum, he drapt out
longer de yuther ripe 'simmons, but time he totch de
groun' he got his foots tergedder, en he lit out fer de
fence same ez a race-hoss, en 'cross dat patch him en
Brer B'ar had it, en Brer B'ar gain' eve'y jump, twel

time Brer Possum make de fence Brer B'ar grab 'im
by de tail, en Brer Possum, he went out 'tween de rails
en gin a powerful juk en pull his tail out 'twix Brer
B'ar tushes; en, lo en beholes,
Brer B'ar hole so tight en
Brer Possum pull so hard
dat all de ha'r come

off in Brer
B'ar's mouf,
w'ich, ef Brer
Rabbit hadnt'
er happen up
wid a go'd er water, Brer B'ar 'der got strankle.

"Fum dat day ter dis," said Uncle Remus,

knocking the ashes carefully out of his pipe, "Brer
Possum ain't had no ha'r on his tail, en needer do
his chilluns."

XXVIII.

THE END OF MR. BEAR.

THE next time the little boy sought Uncle Remus
out, he found the old man unusually cheerful and good-
humoured. His rheumatism had ceased to trouble him,
and he was even disposed to be boisterous. He was
singing when the little boy got near the cabin, and the
child paused on the outside to listen to the vigorous but
mellow voice of the old man, as it rose and fell with
the burden of the curiously plaintive song—a senseless
affair so far as the words were concerned, but sung to a
melody almost thrilling in its sweetness :

> " Han' me down my walkin'-cane
> (Hey my Lily ! go down de road !),
> Yo' true lover gone down de lane
> (Hey my Lily ! go down de road !)."

The quick ear of Uncle Remus, however, had de-
tected the presence of the little boy, and he allowed
his song to run into a recitation of nonsense, of which
the following, if it be rapidly spoken, will give a faint
idea :

" Ole M'er Jackson, fines' confraction, fell down

sta'rs fer to git satisfaction; big Bill Fray, he rule de day, eve'ything he call fer come one, two by three. Gwine 'long one day, met Johnny Huby, ax him grine nine yards er steel fer me, tole me w'ich he couldn't; den I hist 'im over Hickerson Dickerson's barn-doors; knock 'im ninety-nine miles under water, w'en he rise, he rise in Pike straddle un a hanspike, en I lef' 'im dar smokin' er de hornpipe, Juba reda seda breda. Aunt Kate at de gate; I want to eat, she fry de meat en gimme skin, w'ich I fling it back agin. Juba!"

All this, rattled off at a rapid rate and with apparent seriousness, was calculated to puzzle the little boy, and he slipped into his accustomed seat with an expression of awed bewilderment upon his face.

" Hit's all des dat away, honey," continued the old man, with the air of one who had just given an important piece of information. " En w'en you bin cas'n shadders long ez de ole nigger, den you'll fine out who's w'ich, en w'ich's who."

The little boy made no response. He was in thorough sympathy with all the whims and humors of the old man, and his capacity for enjoying them was large enough to include even those he could not understand. Uncle Remus was finishing an axe-handle, and upon these occasions it was his custom to allow the child to hold one end while he applied sand-paper to the other. These relations were pretty soon established, to the mutual satisfaction of the parties most interested, and the old man continued his remarks, but this time not at random :

"W'en I see deze yer swell-head folks like dat 'oman w'at come en tell yo' ma 'bout you chunkin' at her chilluns, w'ich yo' ma make Mars John strop you, hit make my mine run back to ole Brer B'ar. Ole Brer B'ar, he got de swell-headedness hisse'f, en ef der wuz enny swinkin', hit swunk too late fer ter he'p ole Brer B'ar. Leas'ways dat's w'at dey tells me, en I ain't never yearn it 'sputed."

"Was the Bear's head sure enough swelled, Uncle Remus ? "

"Now you talkin', honey ! " exclaimed the old man.

"Goodness ! what made it swell ? "

This was Uncle Remus's cue. Applying the sand-paper to the axe-helve with gentle vigor, he began :

"One time when Brer Rabbit wuz gwine lopin' home fum a frolic w'at dey bin havin' up at Miss Meadows's, who should he happin up wid but ole Brer B'ar. Co'se, atter w'at done pass 'twix um dey wa'n't no good feelin's 'tween Brer Rabbit en ole Brer B'ar, but Brer Rabbit, he wanter save his manners, en so he holler out :

"Heyo, Brer B'ar ! how you come on ? I ain't seed you in a coon's age. How all down at yo' house ? How Miss Brune en Miss Brindle ? "

"Who was that, Uncle Remus ? " the little boy interrupted.

21

"Miss Brune en Miss Brindle? Miss Brune wuz
Brer B'ar's ole 'oman, en Miss Brindle wuz his gal.
Dat w'at dey call um
in dem days. So den
Brer Rabbit, he ax
him howdy, he did,
en Brer B'ar, he 'spon'

dat he wuz mighty po'ly, en dey amble 'long, dey did,
sorter familious like, but Brer Rabbit, he keep one eye
on Brer B'ar, en Brer B'ar, he study how he gwine nab
Brer Babbit. Las' Brer Rabbit, he up'n say, sezee :

"'Brer B'ar, I speck I got some bizness cut out fer
you,' sezee.

"'What dat, Brer Rabbit?' sez Brer B'ar, sezee.

"'W'iles I wuz cleanin' up my new-groun' day 'fo'
yistiddy,' sez Brer Rabbit, sezee, 'I come 'cross wunner
deze yer ole time bee-trees. Hit start holler at de bot-

tom, en stay holler plum der de top, en de honey's des
natally oozin' out, en ef you'll drap yo' 'gagements en
go 'longer me,' sez Brer Rabbit, sezee, ' you'll git a bait
dat'll las' you en yo' fambly twel de
middle er nex' mont',' sezee.

" Brer B'ar say he much
oblije en he b'leeve he'll go
'long, en wid dat dey put out
fer Brer Rabbit's new-groun',
w'ich twa'n't so mighty fur.
Leas'ways, dey got dar atter
w'ile. Ole Brer B'ar, he 'low dat
he kin smell de honey. Brer Rabbit, he 'low dat he kin see de hon-
ey-koam. Brer B'ar, he low dat
he can hear de bees a zoonin'.
Dey stan' 'roun' en talk biggity,
dey did, twel bimeby Brer Rabbit, he up'n say, sezee :

" ' You do de clim-'in', Brer
B'ar, en I'll do de rushin'
'roun'; you clime up ter de
hole, en I'll take dis yer

pine pole en shove de honey up whar you kin git
'er', sezee.

"Ole Brer B'ar, he spit on his han's en skint up de
tree, en jam his head in de hole, en sho nuff, Brer Rabbit, he grab de pine pole, en de way he stir up dem bees
wuz sinful—dat's w'at it wuz. Hit wuz sinful. En de
bees dey swawm'd on Brer B'ar's head, twel 'fo' he could
take it out'n de hole hit wuz done swell up bigger dan
dat dinner-pot, en dar he swung, en ole Brer Rabbit,
he dance 'roun' en sing:

> "'Tree stan' high, but honey mighty sweet—
> Watch dem bees wid stingers on der feet.'

"But dar ole Brer B'ar hung, en ef his head ain't
swunk, I speck he hangin' dar yit—dat w'at I speck."

XXIX.

MR. FOX GETS INTO SERIOUS BUSINESS.

"HIT turn out one time," said Uncle Remus, grind-
ing some crumbs of tobacco between the palms of his
hands, preparatory to enjoying his usual smoke after
supper—"hit turn out one time dat Brer Rabbit make
so free wid de man's collard-patch dat de man he tuck'n
sot a trap fer ole Brer Rabbit."

"Which man was that, Uncle Remus?" asked the
little boy.

" Des a man, honey. Dat's all. Dat's all I knows
—des wunner dese yer mans w'at you see trollopin
'roun' eve'y day. Nobody ain't never year w'at his
name is, en ef dey did dey kep' de news mighty close
fum me. Ef dish yer man is bleedzd fer ter have a
name, den I'm done, kaze you'll hatter go fudder dan
me. Ef you bleedzd ter know mo' dan w'at I duz,
den you'll hatter hunt up some er deze yer niggers
w'at's sprung up sence I commence fer ter shed my
ha'r."

" Well, I just thought, Uncle Remus," said the little
boy, in a tone remarkable for self-depreciation, " that
the man had a name."

" Tooby sho," replied the old man, with unction,
puffing away at his pipe. " Co'se. Dat w'at make I
say w'at I duz. Dish yer man mout a had a name,
en den ag'in he moutn't. He mout er bin name Slip-
shot Sam, en he mouter bin name ole One-eye Riley,
w'ich ef 'twuz hit ain't bin handed roun' ter me. But
dish yer man, he in de tale, en w'at we gwine do wid
'im ? Dat's de p'int, kase w'en I git ter huntin' 'roun'
'mong my 'membunce atter dish yer Mister W'atyou-
maycollum's name, she ain't dar. Now den, less des
call 'im Mr. Man en let 'im go at dat."

The silence of the little boy gave consent.

" One time," said Uncle Remus, carefully taking up
the thread of the story where it had been dropped, " hit
turn out dat Brer Rabbit bin makin' so free wid Mr.

Man's greens en truck dat Mr. Man, he tuck'n sot a trap for Brer Rabbit, en Brer Rabbit he so greedy dat he tuck'n walk right spang in it, 'fo' he know hisse'f. Well, 'twa'n't long 'fo' yer come Mr. Man, broozin' 'roun', en he ain't no sooner see ole Brer Rabbit dan he smack his han's tergedder en holler out:

" ' Youer nice feller, you is! Yer you bin gobblin' up my green truck, en now you tryin' ter tote off my trap. Youer mighty nice chap—dat's w'at you is! But now dat I got you, I'll des 'bout settle wid you fer de ole en de new.'

" En wid dat, Mr. Man, he go off, he did, down in de bushes atter han'ful er switches. Ole Brer Rabbit, he ain't sayin' nuthin', but he feelin' mighty lonesome, en he sot dar lookin' like eve'y minnit wuz gwineter be de nex'. En w'iles Mr. Man wuz off prepa'r'n his bresh-broom, who should come p'radin' 'long but Brer Fox. Brer Fox make a great 'miration, he did, 'bout de fix w'at he fine Brer Rabbit in, but Brer Rabbit he make like he fit ter kill hisse'f laffin', en he up'n tell Brer Fox, he did, dat Miss Meadows's fokes want 'im ter go down ter der house in 'tennunce on a weddin', en he 'low w'ich he couldn't, en dey 'low how he could, en den bimeby dey take'n tie 'im dar w'iles dey go atter de preacher, so he be dar w'en dey come back. En mo'n dat, Brer Rabbit up'n tell Brer Fox dat his chillun's mighty low wid de fever, en he bleedzd ter go atter some pills fer'm, en he ax Brer Fox fer ter take his place en

go down ter Miss Meadows's en have nice time wid
de gals. Brer Fox, he in fer dem kinder pranks, en

'twa'n't no time 'fo'
Brer Rabbit had ole
Brer Fox harness up
dar in his place, en den he make like he got ter
make 'as'e en git de pills fer dem sick chilluns. Brer
Rabbit wa'n't mo'n out er sight 'fo' yer come Mr. Man
wid a han'ful er hick'ries, but w'en he see Brer Fox tied
up dar, he look like he 'stonished.

" ' Heyo !' sez Mr. Man, sezee, ' you done change
color, en you done got bigger, en yo' tail done grow
out. W'at kin'er w'atzyname is you, ennyhow ? ' sezee.

" Brer Fox, he stay still, en Mr. Man, he talk on :

" ' Hit's mighty big luck,' sezee, ' ef w'en I ketch de chap w'at nibble my greens, likewise I ketch de feller w'at gnyaw my goose,' sezee, en wid dat he let inter Brer Fox wid de hick'ries, en de way he play rap-jacket wuz a caution ter de naberhood. Brer Fox, he juk en he jump, en he squeal en he squall, but Mr. Man, he shower down on 'im, he did, like fightin' a red was'-nes'.' "

The little boy laughed, and Uncle Remus supplemented this indorsement of his descriptive powers with a most infectious chuckle.

" Bimeby," continued the old man, " de switches, dey got frazzle out, en Mr. Man, he put out atter mo', en w'en he done got fa'rly outer yearin', Brer Rabbit, he show'd up, he did, kaze he des bin hidin' out in de bushes lis'nin' at de racket, en he 'low hit mighty funny dat Miss Meadows ain't come 'long, kaze he done bin down ter de doctor house, en dat's fudder dan de preacher, yit. Brer Rabbit make like he hurr'in' on home, but Brer Fox, he open up, he did, en he say :

" ' I thank you fer ter tu'n me loose, Brer Rabbit, en I'll be 'blije,' sezee, ' kaze you done tie me up so tight dat it make my head swim, en I don't speck I'd las' fer ter git ter Miss Meadows's', sezee.

" Brer Rabbit, he sot down sorter keerless like, en begin fer ter scratch one year like a man studyin' 'bout sump'n.

" ' Dat's so, Brer Fox,' sezee, ' you duz look sorter

stove up.   Look like sump'n bin onkoamin' yo' ha'rs,' sezee.

"Brer Fox ain't sayin' nothin', but Brer Rabbit, he keep on talkin':

"'Dey ain't no bad feelin's 'twix' us, is dey, Brer Fox? Kaze ef dey is, I ain't got no time fer ter be tarryin' 'roun' yer.'

"Brer Fox say w'ich he don't have no onfrennelness, en wid dat Brer Rabbit cut Brer Fox loose des in time fer ter hear Mr. Man w'isserlin up his dogs, en one went one way en de udder went nudder."

XXX.

HOW MR. RABBIT SUCCEEDED IN RAISING A DUST.

"In dem times," said Uncle Remus, gazing admiringly at himself in a fragment of looking-glass, "Brer Rabbit, en Brer Fox, en Brer Coon, en dem yuther creeturs go co'tin' en sparklin' 'roun' de naberhood mo' samer dan folks. 'Twan't no 'Lemme a hoss,' ner 'Fetch me my buggy,' but dey des up'n lit out en tote deyse'f. Dar's ole Brer Fox, he des wheel 'roun' en fetch his flank one swipe wid 'is tongue en he'd be koam up; en Brer Rabbit, he des spit on his han' en twis' it 'roun' 'mongst de roots er his years en his ha'r'd be roach. Dey wuz dat flirtashus," continued the old man, closing one eye at his image in the glass, "dat Miss Meadows en de gals don't se no peace fum one week een' ter de udder. Chuseday wuz same as Sunday, en Friday wuz same as Chuseday, en hit come down ter dat pass dat w'en Miss Meadows 'ud have chicken-fixins fer dinner, in 'ud drap Brer Fox en Brer Possum, en w'en she'd have fried greens in 'ud pop ole Brer Rabbit, twel 'las' Miss Meadows, she tuck'n tell de gals dat she be dad-blame ef she gwineter keep no tavvum. So dey fix it up 'mong deyse'f, Miss Meadows en de gals did, dat de nex' time de gents call dey'd gin um a game. De gents, dey wuz a co'tin, but Miss Meadows, she don't wanter marry none un um, en needer duz de gals, en likewise dey don't wanter have um pester'n 'roun'. Las', one Chuseday, Miss Meadows, she tole um dat ef dey come down ter her house de nex' Sat'day evenin', de whole caboodle un um 'ud go down de road a piece, whar der wuz a big flint rock, en de man w'at could take a sludge-hammer en knock de dus' out'n dat rock, he wuz de man w'at 'ud git de pick er de gals. Dey all say dey gwine do it, but ole Brer Rabbit, he crope off whar der wuz a cool place under some jimson weeds, en dar he sot wukkin his mind how he gwineter git dus' out'n dat rock. Bime-by, w'ile he wuz a settin' dar, up he jump en crack his heels tergedder en sing out:

> " ' Make a bow ter de Buzzard en
> den ter de Crow,
> Takes a limber-toe gemmun fer
> ter jump Jim Crow,'

en wid dat he put out for Brer Coon house en borrer his slippers. W'en Sat'day evenin' come, dey wuz all dere. Miss Meadows en de gals, dey wuz dere; en Brer Coon, en Brex Fox, en Brer Possum, en Brer Tarrypin, dey wuz dere."

" Where was the Rabbit ?" the little boy asked.

" Youk'n put yo' 'pennunce in ole Brer Rabbit,"

the old man replied, with a chuckle. "He wuz dere, but he shuffle up kinder late, kaze w'en Miss Meadows en de ballunce un um done gone down ter de place, Brer Rabbit, he crope 'roun' ter de ash-hopper, en fill Brer Coon slippers full er ashes, en den he tuck'n put um on en march off. He got dar atter 'w'ile, en soon's Miss Meadows en de gals seed 'im, dey up'n giggle, en make a great 'miration kaze Brer Rabbit got on slippers. Brer Fox, he so smart, he holler out, he did, en say he lay Brer Rabbit got de groun'-eatch,' but Brer Rabbit, he sorter shet one eye, he did, en say, sezee :

" 'I bin so useter ridin' hoss-back, ez deze ladies knows, dat I'm gittin' sorter tender-footed ; ' en dey don't hear much mo' fum Brer Fox dat day, kaze he 'member how Brer Rabbit done bin en rid him ; en hit 'uz des 'bout much ez Miss Meadows en de gals could do fer ter keep der snickers fum gittin' up a 'sturbance 'mong de congergashun. But, never mine dat, old Brer Rabbit, he wuz dar, en he so brash dat leetle mo' en he'd er grab up de sludge-hammer en er open up de racket 'fo' ennybody gun de word ; but Brer Fox, he shove Brer Rabbit out'n de way en pick up de sludge hisse'f. Now den," continued the old man, with pretty much the air of one who had been the master of similar ceremonies, "de progance wuz dish yer : Eve'y gent wer ter have th'ee licks at de rock, en de gent w'at fetch de dus' he wer de one w'at gwineter take de pick er de gals. Ole Brer Fox, he grab de sludge-hammer, he did,

en he come down on de rock—*blim!* No dus' ain't
come. Den he draw back en down he come ag'in—
blam! No dus' ain't come.
Den he spit in his han's, en

give 'er a big swing
en down she come—*ker-
blap!* En yit no dus'
ain't flew'd. Den Brer Possum he make triul, en
Brer Coon, en all de ballunce un um 'cep' Brer Tarrypin, en he 'low dat he got a crick in his neck.
Den Brer Rabbit, he grab holt er de sludge, en he lipt
up in de a'r en come down on de rock all at de same
time—*pow!*—en de ashes, dey flew'd up so, dey did,

dat Brer Fox, he tuck'n had a sneezin' spell, en Miss
Meadows en de gals dey up'n koff.   Th'ee times Brer
Rabbit jump up en crack his heels tergedder en come
down   wid   de   sludge-hammer—*ker-blam !*—en   eve'y
time he jump up, he holler out :

"'Stan' fudder, ladies !   Yer come de dus'!' en sho
nuff, de dus' come.

"Leas'ways," continued Uncle Remus, "Brer Rabbit got one er de gals, en dey had a weddin' en a big
infa'r."

"Which of the girls did the Rabbit marry ?" asked
the little boy, dubiously.

"I did year tell un 'er name," replied the old man,
with a great affectation of interest, "but look like I
done gone en fergit it off'n my mine.   Ef I don't dis-
remember," he continued, "hit wuz Miss Molly Cotton-
tail, en I speck we better let it go at dat."

XXXI.

A PLANTATION WITCH.

THE next time the little boy got permission to call
upon Uncle Remus, the old man was sitting in his
door, with his elbows on his knees and his face
buried in his hands, and he appeared to be in great
trouble.

"What's the matter, Uncle Remus?" the youngster asked.

"Nuff de matter, honey—mo' dan dey's enny kyo fer. Ef dey ain't some quare gwines on 'roun' dis place I ain't name Remus."

The serious tone of the old man caused the little boy to open his eyes. The moon, just at its full, cast long, vague, wavering shadows in front of the cabin. A colony of tree-frogs somewhere in the distance were treating their neighbors to a serenade, but to the little boy it sounded like a chorus of lost and long-forgotten whistlers. The sound was wherever the imagination chose to locate it—to the right, to the left, in the air, on the ground, far away or near at hand, but always dim and always indistinct. Something in Uncle Remus's tone exactly fitted all these surroundings, and the child nestled closer to the old man.

"Yasser," continued Uncle Remus, with an ominous sigh and mysterious shake of the head, "ef dey ain't some quare gwines on in dish yer naberhood, den I'm de ball-headest creetur 'twix' dis en nex' Jinawerry wuz a year 'go, w'ich I knows I ain't. Dat's what."

"What is it, Uncle Remus?"

"I know Mars John bin drivin' Cholly sorter hard ter-day, en I say ter myse'f dat I'd drap 'roun' 'bout dus' en fling nudder year er corn in de troff en kinder gin 'im a techin' up wid de kurrier-koam; en bless grashus! I ain't bin in de lot mo'n a minnit 'fo' I seed sump'n wuz wrong wid de hoss, and sho' nuff dar wuz his mane full er witch-stirrups."

" Full of what, Uncle Remus ? "

" Full er witch-stirrups, honey. Ain't you seed no witch-stirrups ? Well, w'en you see two stran' er ha'r tied tergedder in a hoss's mane, dar you see a witch-stirrup, en, mo'n dat, dat hoss done bin rid by um."

" Do you reckon they have been riding Charley ? " inquired the little boy.

" Co'se, honey. Tooby sho dey is. W'at else dey bin doin' ? "

" Did you ever see a witch, Uncle Remus ? "

" Dat ain't needer yer ner dar. W'en I see coon track in de branch, I know de coon bin 'long dar."

The argument seemed unanswerable, and the little boy asked, in a confidential tone :

" Uncle Remus, what are witches like ? "

" Dey comes diffunt," responded the cautious old darkey. "Dey comes en dey cunjus fokes. Squinch-owl holler eve'y time he see a witch, en w'en you hear de dog howlin' in de middle er de night, one un um's mighty ap' ter be prowlin' 'roun'. Cunjun fokes kin tell a witch de minnit dey lays der eyes on it, but dem w'at ain't cunjun, hit's mighty hard ter tell w'en dey see one, kaze dey might

come ín de 'pearunce un a cow en all kinder creeturs. I ain't bin useter no cunjun myse'f, but I bin
livin' long nuff fer ter know w'en you meets up wid
a big black cat in de middle er de road, wid yaller
eyeballs, dars yo' witch fresh
fum de Ole Boy. En, fudder-
mo', I know dat 'tain't

proned
inter no
dogs fer
ter ketch de rabbit
w'at use in a berryin'-
groun'. Dey er de mos' ongodlies' creeturs w'at you
ever laid eyes on," continued Uncle Remus, with unction. "Down dar in Putmon County yo' Unk Jeems,
he make like he gwineter ketch wunner dem dar grave-
yard rabbits. Sho nuff, out he goes, en de dogs ain't

no mo'n got ter de place fo' up jump de old rabbit right
'mong um, en atter runnin' 'roun' a time or two, she
skip right up ter Mars Jeems, en Mars Jeems, he des
put de gun-bairl right on 'er en lammed aloose. Hit
tored up de groun' all 'roun', en de dogs, dey rush up,
but dey wa'n't no rabbit dar ; but bimeby Mars Jeems,
he seed de dogs tuckin' der tails 'tween der legs, en he
look up, en dar wuz de rabbit caperin' 'roun' on a toom-
stone, en wid dat Mars Jeems say he sorter feel like de
time done come w'en yo' gran'ma was 'specktin' un him
home, en he call off de dogs en put out. But dem wuz
ha'nts. Witches is deze yer kinder fokes wat kin drap
der body en change inter a cat en a wolf en all kinder
creeturs."

"Papa says there ain't any witches," the little boy
interrupted.

"Mars John ain't live long ez I is," said Uncle
Remus, by way of comment. "He ain't bin broozin'
'roun' all hours er de night en day. I know'd a nigger
w'ich his brer wuz a witch, kaze he up'n tole me how
he tuck'n kyo'd 'im ; en he kyo'd 'im good, mon."

"How was that ?" inquired the little boy.

"Hit seem like," continued Uncle Remus, "dat
witch fokes is got a slit in de back er de neck, en w'en
dey wanter change derse'f, dey des pull de hide over
der head same ez if 'twuz a shut, en dar dey is."

"Do they get out of their skins?" asked the little
boy, in an awed tone.

"Tooby sho, honey. You see yo' pa pull his shut off? Well, dat dez 'zackly de way dey duz. But dish yere nigger w'at I'm tellin' you 'bout, he kyo'd his brer de ve'y fus pass he made at him. Hit got so dat fokes in de settlement didn't have no peace. De chilluns 'ud wake up in de mawnins wid der ha'r tangle up, en wid scratches on um like dey bin thoo a brier-patch, twel bimeby one day de nigger he 'low dat he'd set up dat night en keep one eye on his brer; en sho' nuff dat night, des ez de chickens wuz crowin' fer twelve, up jump de brer an pull off his skin en sail out'n de house in de shape un a bat, en w'at duz de nigger do but grab up de hide, en turn it wrongsudout'ards en sprinkle it wid salt. Den he lay down en watch fer ter see w'at de news wuz gwineter be. Des 'fo' day yer come a big black cat in de do', en de nigger git up, he did, en druv her away. Bimeby, yer come a big black dog snuffin' roun', en de nigger up wid a chunk en lammed 'im side er de head. Den a squinch-owl lit on de koam er de house, en de nigger jam de shovel in de fier en make 'im flew away. Las', yer come a great big black wolf wid his eyes shinin' like fier coals, en he grab de hide and rush out. 'Twa'n't long 'fo' de nigger year his brer holler'n en squallin', en he tuck a light, he did, en went out, en dar wuz his brer des a waller'n on de groun' en squirmin' 'roun', kaze de salt on de skin wuz stingin' wuss'n ef he had his britches lineded wid yaller-jackets. By nex' mawnin' he got so he could

sorter shuffle 'long, but he gun up cunjun, en ef dere
wuz enny mo' witches in dat settlement dey kep'
mighty close, en dat nigger he ain't skunt hisse'f no
mo' not endurin' er my 'membunce."

The result of this was that Uncle Remus had to
take the little boy by the hand and go with him to
the "big house," which the old man was not loath to
do; and, when the child went to bed, he lay awake a
long time expecting an unseemly visitation from some
mysterious source. It soothed him, however, to hear
the strong, musical voice of his sable patron, not very
far away, tenderly contending with a lusty tune; and
to this accompaniment the little boy dropped asleep:

> " Hit's eighteen hunder'd, forty-en-eight,
> Christ done made dat crooked way straight—
>   En I don't wanter stay here no longer;
> Hit's eighteen hunder'd, forty-en-nine,
> Christ done turn dat water inter wine—
>   En I don't wanter stay here no longer."

XXXII.

"JACKY-MY-LANTERN."*

UPON his next visit to Uncle Remus, the little boy
was exceedingly anxious to know more about witches,

---

* This story is popular on the coast and among the rice-planta-
tions, and, since the publication of some of the animal-myths in the

but the old man prudently refrained from exciting the youngster's imagination any further in that direction. Uncle Remus had a board across his lap, and, armed with a mallet and a shoe-knife, was engaged in making shoe-pegs.

"W'iles I wuz crossin' de branch des now," he said, endeavoring to change the subject, "I come up wid a Jacky-my-lantern, en she wuz bu'nin' wuss'n a bunch er lightnin'-bugs, mon. I know'd she wuz a fixin' fer ter lead me inter dat quogmire down in de swamp, en I steer'd cle'r un 'er. Yasser. I did dat. You ain't never seed no Jacky-my-lanterns, is you, honey?"

The little boy never had, but he had heard of them, and he wanted to know what they were, and thereupon Uncle Remus proceeded to tell him.

"One time," said the old darkey, transferring his spectacles from his nose to the top of his head and leaning his elbows upon his peg-board, "dere wuz a blacksmif man, en dish yer blacksmif man, he tuck'n stuck closer by his dram dan he did by his bellus. Monday mawnin' he'd git on a spree, en all dat week he'd be on a spree, en de nex' Monday mawnin' he'd take a fresh start. Bimeby, one day, atter de black-

newspapers, I have received a version of it from a planter in south-west Georgia; but it seems to me to be an intruder among the genuine myth-stories of the negroes. It is a trifle too elaborate. Nevertheless, it is told upon the plantations with great gusto, and there are several versions in circulation.

smif bin spreein' 'roun' en cussin' might'ly, he hear a
sorter rustlin' fuss at de do', en in walk de Bad Man."

"Who, Uncle Remus?" the little boy asked.

"De Bad Man, honey; de Ole Boy hisse'f right
fresh from de ridjun w'at you year Miss Sally readin'
'bout. He done hide his hawns, en his tail, en his
hoof, en he come dress up like w'ite fokes. He tuck
off his hat en he bow, en den he tell de blacksmif who
he is, en dat he done come atter 'im. Den de blacksmif, he gun ter cry en beg, en he beg so hard en he
cry so loud dat de Bad Man say he make a trade wid
'im. At de een' er one year de sperit er de blacksmif
wuz to be his'n en endurin' er dat time de blacksmif
mus' put in his hottes' licks in de intruss er de Bad
Man, en den he put a spell on de cheer de blacksmif
was settin' in, en on his sludge-hammer. De man
w'at sot in de cheer couldn't git up less'n de blacksmif let 'im, en de man w'at pick up de sludge 'ud
hatter keep on knockin' wid it twel de blacksmif say
quit; en den he gun 'im money plenty, en off he put.

"De blacksmif, he sail in fer ter have his fun, en he
have so much dat he done clean forgot 'bout his con-
track, but bimeby, one day he look down de road, en
dar he see de Bad Man comin', en den he know'd de
year wuz out. W'en de Bad Man got in de do', de
blacksmif wuz poundin' 'way at a hoss-shoe, but he
wa'n't so bizzy dat he didn't ax 'im in. De Bad Man
sorter do like he ain't got no time fer ter tarry, but de

blacksmif say he got some little jobs dat he bleedzd ter
finish up, en den he ax de Bad Man fer ter set down a
minnit; en de Bad Man, he
tuck'n sot down, en he sot
in dat cheer w'at he
done conju'd en,
co'se, dar he
wuz. Den de
black-
smif,

he 'gun ter poke
fun at de Bad Man,
en he ax him don't he
want a dram, en won't he hitch his cheer up little
nigher de fier, en de Bad Man, he beg en he beg,
but 'twan't doin' no good, kase de blacksmif 'low
dat he gwineter keep 'im dar twel he promus dat he
let 'im off one year mo', en, sho nuff, de Bad Man
promus dat ef de blacksmif let 'im up he give 'im

a n'er showin'. So den de blacksmif gun de wud, en de Bad Man sa'nter off down de big road, settin' traps en layin' his progance fer ter ketch mo' sinners.

"De nex' year hit pass same like t'er one. At de 'p'inted time yer come de Ole Boy atter de blacksmif, but still de blacksmif had some jobs dat he bleedzd ter finish up, en he ax de Bad Man fer ter take holt er de sludge en he'p 'im out; en de Bad Man, he 'low dat r'er'n be disperlite, he don't keer ef he do hit 'er a biff er two; en wid dat he grab up de sludge, en dar he wuz 'gin, kase he done conju'd de sludge so dat whosomedever tuck 'er up can't put 'er down less'n de blacksmif say de wud. Dey perlaver'd dar, dey did, twel bimeby de Bad Man he up'n let 'im off n'er year.

"Well, den, dat year pass same ez t'er one. Mont' in en mont' out dat man wuz rollin' in dram, en bimeby yer come de Bad Man. De blacksmif cry en he holler, en he rip 'roun' en t'ar his ha'r, but hit des like he didn't, kase de Bad Man grab 'im up en cram 'im in a bag en tote 'im off. W'iles dey wuz gwine 'long dey come up wid a passel er fokes w'at wuz havin' wunner deze yer fote er July bobbycues, en de Ole Boy, he 'low dat maybe he kin git some mo' game, en w'at do he do but jine in wid um. He jines in en he talk politics same like t'er fokes, twel bimeby dinnertime come 'roun', en dey ax 'im up, w'ich 'greed wid his stummuck, en he pozzit his bag underneed de table 'longside de udder bags w'at de hongry fokes'd brung.

"No sooner did de blacksmif git back on de groun' dan he 'gun ter wuk his way outer de bag. He crope out, he did, en den he tuck'n change de bag. He tuck'n tuck a n'er bag en lay it down whar dish yer bag wuz, en den he crope outer de crowd en lay low in de underbresh.

"Las', w'en de time come fer ter go, de Ole Boy up wid his bag en slung her on his shoulder, en off he put fer de Bad Place. W'en he got dar he tuck'n drap de bag off'n his back en call up de imps, en dey des come a squallin' en a caperin', w'ich I speck dey mus' a bin hongry. Leas'ways dey des swawm'd 'roun', hollerin out:

"'Daddy, w'at you brung—daddy, w'at you brung?'

"So den dey open de bag, en lo en beholes, out jump a big bull-dog, en de way he shuck dem little imps wuz a caution, en he kep' on gnyawin' un um twel de Ole Boy open de gate en tu'n 'im out."

"And what became of the blacksmith?" the little boy asked, as Uncle Remus paused to suuff the candle with his fingers.

"I'm drivin' on 'roun', honey. Atter 'long time, de blacksmif he tuck'n die, en w'en he go ter de Good Place de man at de gate dunner who he is, en he can't squeeze in. Den he go down ter de Bad Place, en knock. De Ole Boy, he look out, he did, en he know'd de blacksmif de minnit he laid eyes on 'im; but he shake his head en say, sezee:

"'You'll hatter skuze me, Brer Blacksmif, kase I dun had 'speunce 'longer you. You'll hatter go some'rs else ef you wanter raise enny racket,' sezee, en wid dat he shet de do'.

"En dey do say," continued Uncle Remus, with unction, "dat sence dat day de blacksmif bin sorter huv'rin' 'roun' 'twix' de heavens en de ye'th, en dark nights he shine out so fokes call 'im Jacky-my-lantun. Dat's w'at dey tells me. Hit may be wrong er't maybe right, but dat's w'at I years."

XXXIII.

WHY THE NEGRO IS BLACK.

ONE night, while the little boy was watching Uncle Remus twisting and waxing some shoe-thread, he made what appeared to him to be a very curious discovery. He discovered that the palms of the old man's hands were as white as his own, and the fact was such a source of wonder that he at last made it the subject of remark. The response of Uncle Remus led to the earnest recital of a piece of unwritten history that must prove interesting to ethnologists.

"Tooby sho de pa'm er my han's w'ite, honey," he quietly remarked, "en, w'en it come ter dat, dey wuz a time w'en all de w'ite folks 'uz black—blacker dan me, kaze I done bin yer so long dat I bin sorter bleach out."

The little boy laughed. He thought Uncle Remus was making him the victim of one of his jokes; but the youngster was never more mistaken. The old man was serious. Nevertheless, he failed to rebuke the ill-timed mirth of the child, appearing to be altogether engrossed in his work. After a while he resumed:

"Yasser. Fokes dunner w'at bin yit, let 'lone w'at gwineter be. Niggers is niggers now, but de time wuz w'en we 'uz all niggers tergedder."

"When was that, Uncle Remus?"

"Way back yander. In dem times we 'uz all un us black; we 'uz all niggers tergedder, en 'cordin' ter all de 'counts w'at I years fokes 'uz gittin' 'long 'bout ez well in dem days ez dey is now. But atter 'w'ile de news come dat dere wuz a pon' er water some'rs in de naberhood, w'ich ef dey'd git inter dey'd be wash off nice en w'ite, en den one un um, he fine de place en make er splunge inter de pon', en come out w'ite ez a town gal. En den, bless grashus! w'en de fokes seed it, dey make a break fer de pon', en dem w'at wuz de soopless, dey got in fus' en dey come out w'ite; en dem w'at wuz de nex' soopless, dey got in nex', en dey come out merlatters; en dey wuz sech a crowd un um dat dey mighty nigh use de water up, w'ich w'en dem yuthers come 'long, de morest dey could do wuz ter paddle about wid der foots en dabble in it wid der han's. Dem wuz de niggers, en down ter dis day dey ain't no w'ite 'bout a nigger 'ceppin de pa'ms er der han's en de soles er der foot."

The little boy seemed to be very much interested in this new account of the origin of races, and he made some further inquiries, which elicited from Uncle Remus the following additional particulars:

"De Injun en de Chinee got ter be 'counted 'long er de merlatter. I ain't seed no Chinee dat I knows un, but dey tells me dey er sorter 'twix' a brown en a brindle. Dey er all merlatters."

"But mamma says the Chinese have straight hair," the little boy suggested.

"Co'se, honey," the old man unhesitatingly responded, "dem w'at git ter de pon' time nuff fer ter git der head in de water, de water hit onkink der ha'r. Hit bleedzd ter be dat away."

XXXIV.

THE SAD FATE OF MR. FOX.

"Now, den," said Uncle Remus, with unusual gravity, as soon as the little boy, by taking his seat, announced that he was ready for the evening's entertainment to begin; "now, den, dish yer tale w'at I'm agwine ter gin you is de las' row er stumps, sho. Dish yer's whar ole Brer Fox los' his breff, en he ain't fine it no mo' down ter dis day."

"Did he kill himself, Uncle Remus?" the little boy asked, with a curious air of concern.

"Hole on dar, honey!" the old man exclaimed, with a great affectation of alarm; "hole on dar! Wait! Gimme room! I don't wanter tell you no story, en ef you keep shovin' me forrerd, I mout git some er de facks mix up 'mong deyse'f. You gotter gimme room en you gotter gimme time."

The little boy had no other premature ques-

tions to ask, and, after a pause, Uncle Remus resumed :

"Well, den, one day Brer Rabbit go ter Brer Fox
house, he did, en he put up mighty po' mouf. He say
his ole 'oman sick, en his chilluns cole, en de fier done
gone out. Brer Fox, he feel bad 'bout dis, en he tuck'n
s'ply Brer Rabbit widder chunk er fier. Brer Rabbit
see Brer Fox cookin' some nice beef, en his mouf gun
ter water, but he take de fier, he did, en he put out
to'rds home ; but present'y yer he come back, en he say
de fier done gone out. Brer Fox 'low dat he want er
invite to dinner, but he don't say nuthin', en bimeby
Brer Rabbit he up'n say, sezee :

" ' Brer Fox, whar you git so much nice beef ? '
sezee, en den Brer Fox he up'n 'spon', sezee :

" ' You come ter my house ter-morrer ef yo' fokes
ain't too sick, en I kin show you whar you kin git
plenty beef mo' nicer dan dish yer,' sezee :

"Well, sho nuff, de nex' day fotch Brer Rabbit, en
Brer Fox say, sezee :

" ' Der's a man down yander by Miss Meadows's
w'at got heap er fine cattle, en he gotter cow name
Bookay,' sezee, 'en you des go en say *Bookay*, en she'll
open her mouf, en you kin jump in en git des as much
meat ez you kin tote,' sez Brer Fox, sezee.

" ' Well, I'll go 'long,' sez Brer Rabbit, sezee, ' en
you kin jump fus' en den I'll come follerin' atter,' sezee.

"Wid dat dey put out, en dey went promernadin'

'roun' 'mong de cattle, dey did, twel bimeby dey struck
up wid de one dey wuz atter.   Brer Fox, he up, he did,

en holler *Boo-
kay*, en de
cow flung 'er
mouf wide
open. Sho nuff,
in dey jump,
en w'en dey got
dar, Brer Fox,
he say, sezee:
" 'You kin
cut mos' enny-
wheres, Brer Rabbit, but don't cut 'roun' de haslett,'
sezee.

" Den Brer Rabbit, he holler back, he did: 'I'm a
gitten me out a roas'n-piece,' sezee.

" 'Roas'n, er bakin', er fryin',' sez Brer Fox, sezee,
'don't git too nigh de haslett,' sezee.

" Dey cut en dey kyarved, en dey kyarved en dey
cut, en w'iles dey wuz cuttin' en kyarvin', en slashin'
'way, Brer Rabbit, he tuck'n hacked inter de haslett,
en wid dat down fell de cow dead.

" ' Now, den,' sez Brer Fox, ' we er gone, sho,'
sezee.

" ' W'at we gwine do ? ' sez Brer Rabbit, sezee.

" ' I'll git in de maul,' sez Brer Fox, ' en you'll
jump in de gall,' sezee.

" Nex' mawnin' yer cum de man w'at de cow
b'long ter, an he ax who kill Bookay. Nobody don't
say nuthin'. Den de man say he'll cut 'er open en see,
en den he whirl in, en twan't no time 'fo' he had 'er
intruls spread out. Brer Rabbit, he crope out'n de
gall, en say, sezee :

" ' Mister Man ! Oh, Mister Man ! I'll tell you
who kill yo' cow. You look in de maul, en dar you'll
fine 'im,' sezee.

" Wid dat de man tuck a stick and lam down on de
maul so hard dat he kill Brer Fox stone-dead. W'en
Brer Rabbit see Brer Fox wuz laid out fer good, he
make like he mighty sorry, en he up'n ax de man fer
Brer Fox head. Man say he ain't keerin', en den Brer
Rabbit tuck'n brung it ter Brer Fox house. Dar he
see ole Miss Fox, en he tell 'er dat he done fotch her
some nice beef w'at 'er ole man sont 'er, but she ain't
gotter look at it twel she go ter eat it.

" Brer Fox son wuz name Tobe, en Brer Rabbit tell
Tobe fer ter keep still w'iles his mammy cook de nice
beef w'at his daddy sont 'im. Tobe he wuz mighty
hongry, en he look in de pot he did w'iles de cookin'
wuz gwine on, en dar he see his daddy head, en wid

dat he sot up a howl en tole his mammy. Miss Fox,
she git mighty mad w'en she fine she cookin' her ole
man head, en she call up de dogs, she did, en sickt em
on Brer Rabbit; en ole Miss Fox en Tobe en de dogs,
dey push Brer Rabbit so close dat he hatter take a
holler tree. Miss Fox, she tell Tobe fer ter stay dar
en mine Brer Rabbit, w'ile she goes en git de ax, en
w'en she gone, Brer Rabbit, he tole Tobe ef he go ter
de branch en git 'im a drink er water dat he'll gin 'im a
dollar. Tobe, he put out, he did, en bring some water
in his hat, but by de time he got back Brer Rabbit
done out en gone. Ole Miss Fox, she cut and cut twel
down come de tree, but no Brer Rabbit dar. Den she
lay de blame on Tobe, en she say she gwineter lash
'im, en Tobe, he put out en run, de ole 'oman atter
'im. Bimeby, he come up wid Brer Rabbit, en sot
down fer to tell 'im how 'twuz, en w'iles dey wuz a
settin' dar, yer come ole Miss Fox a slippin' up en
grab um bofe. Den she tell um w'at she gwine do.
Brer Rabbit she gwineter kill, en Tobe she gwineter
lam ef its de las' ack. Den Brer Rabbit sez, sezee:

"'Ef you please, ma'am, Miss Fox, lay me on de
grinestone en groun' off my nose so I can't smell no
mo' w'en I'm dead.'

"Miss Fox, she tuck dis ter be a good idee, en she
fotch bofe un um ter de grinestone, en set um up on
it so dat she could groun' off Brer Rabbit nose. Den
Brer Rabbit, he up'n say, sezee:

" ' Ef you please, ma'am, Miss Fox, Tobe he kin turn de handle w'iles you goes atter some water fer ter wet de grinestone,' sezee.

" Co'se, soon'z Brer Rabbit see Miss Fox go

atter de water, he jump down en put out, en dis time he git clean away."

" And was that the last of the Rabbit, too, Uncle Remus ? " the little boy asked, with something like a sigh.

" Don't push me too close, honey," responded the old man ; " don't shove me up in no cornder. I don't wanter tell you no stories. Some say dat Brer Rab-

bit's ole 'oman died fum eatin' some pizen-weed, en dat
Brer Rabbit married ole Miss Fox, en some say not.
Some tells one tale en some tells nudder; some say dat
fum dat time forrer'd de Rabbits en de Foxes make
frien's en stay so; some say dey kep on quollin'. Hit
look like it mixt. Let dem tell you w'at knows. Dat
w'at I years you gits it straight like I yeard it."

There was a long pause, which was finally broken
by the old man:

"Hit's 'gin de rules fer you ter be noddin' yer,
honey. Bimeby you'll drap off en I'll hatter tote you
up ter de big 'ouse. I hear dat baby cryin', en bimeby
Miss Sally'll fly up en be a holler'n atter you."

"Oh, I wasn't asleep," the little boy replied. "I
was just thinking."

"Well, dat's diffunt," said the old man. "Ef
you'll clime up on my back," he continued, speaking
softly, "I speck I ain't too ole fer ter be yo' hoss fum
yer ter de house. Many en many's de time dat I toted
yo' Unk Jeems dat away, en Mars Jeems wuz heavier
sot dan w'at you is."

PLANTATION PROVERBS.

Big 'possum clime little tree.
Dem w'at eats kin say grace.
Ole man Know-All died las' year.
Better de gravy dan no grease 'tall.
Dram ain't good twel you git it.
Lazy fokes' stummucks don't git tired.
Rheumatiz don't he'p at de log-rollin'

(173)

Mole don't see w'at his naber doin'.

Save de pacin' mar' fer Sunday.

Don't rain eve'y time de pig squeal.

Crow en corn can't grow in de same fiel'.

Tattlin' 'oman can't make de bread rise.

Rails split 'fo' bre'kfus' 'll season de˙dinner.

Dem w'at knows too much sleeps under de ash-hopper.

Ef you wanter see yo' own sins, clean up a new groun'.

Hog dunner w'ich part un 'im'll season de turnip salad.

Hit's a blessin' de w'ite sow don't shake de plum-tree.

Winter grape sour, whedder you kin reach 'im or not.

Mighty po' bee dat don't make mo' honey dan he want.

Kwishins on mule's foots done gone out er fashun.

Pigs dunno w'at a pen's fer.

Possum's tail good as a paw.

Dogs don't bite at de front gate.

Colt in de barley-patch kick high.

Jay-bird don't rob his own nes'.

Pullet can't roost too high for de owl.

Meat fried 'fo' day won't las' twel night.

Stump water won't kyo de gripes.

De howlin' dog know w'at he sees.

Bline hoss don't fall w'en he follers de bit.

Hongry nigger won't w'ar his maul out.

Don't fling away de empty wallet.

Black-snake know de way ter de hin nes'.

Looks won't do ter split rails wid.

Settin' hens don't hanker arter fresh aigs.

Tater-vine growin' w'ile you sleep.

Hit take two birds fer to make a nes'.

Ef you bleedzd ter eat dirt, eat clean dirt.

Tarrypin walk fast 'nuff fer to go visitin'.

Empty smoke-house makes de pullet holler.

W'en coon take water he fixin' fer ter fight.

Corn makes mo' at de mill dan it does in de crib.

Good luck say : " Op'n yo' mouf en shet yo' eyes."

Nigger dat gets hurt wukkin oughter show de skyars.

Fiddlin' nigger say hit's long ways ter de dance.

Rooster makes mo' racket dan de hin w'at lay de aig.

Meller mush-million hollers at you fum over de fence.

Nigger wid a pocket-han'kcher better be looked atter.

Rain-crow don't sing no chune, but youk'n 'pen' on 'im.

One-eyed mule can't be handled on de bline side.

Moon may shine, but a lightered knot's mighty handy.

Licker talks mighty loud w'en it git loose fum de jug.

De proudness un a man don't count w'en his head's cold.

Hongry rooster don't cackle w'en he fine a wum.

Some niggers mighty smart, but dey can't drive de pidgins ter roos'.

You may know de way, but better keep yo' eyes on de seven stairs.

All de buzzards in de settlement 'll come to de gray mule's funer'l.

Youk'n hide de fier, but w'at you gwine do wid de smoke?

Ter-morrow may be de carridge-driver's day for ploughin'.

Hit's a mighty deaf nigger dat don't year de dinner-ho'n.

Hit takes a bee fer ter git de sweetness out'n de hoar-houn' blossom.

Ha'nts don't bodder longer hones' folks, but you better go 'roun' de grave-yard.

De pig dat runs off wid de year er corn gits little mo' dan de cob.

Sleepin' in de fence-corner don't fetch Chrismus in de kitchen.

De spring-house may freeze, but de niggers 'll keep de shuck-pen warm.

'Twix' de bug en de bee-martin 'tain't hard ter tell w'ich gwineter git kotch.

Don't 'spute wid de squinch-owl.   Jam de shovel in de fier.

You'd see mo' er de mink ef he know'd whar de yard dog sleeps.

Troubles is seasonin'.   'Simmons ain't good twel dey 'er fros'-bit.

Watch out w'en you'er gittin all you want.   Fattenin' hogs ain't in luck.

HIS SONGS.

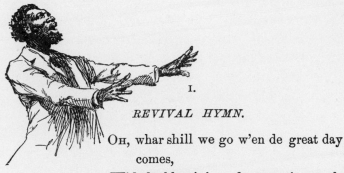

I.

REVIVAL HYMN.

Oh, whar shill we go w'en de great day
 comes,
  Wid de blowin' er de trumpits en de
  bangin' er de drums?
How many po' sinners'll be kotched out late
En fine no latch ter de golden gate?
  No use fer ter wait twel ter-morrer!
  De sun musn't set on yo' sorrer,
  Sin's ez sharp ez a bamboo-brier—
  Oh, Lord! fetch de mo'ners up higher!

W'en de nashuns er de earf is a stan'in all aroun',
Who's a gwineter be choosen fer ter w'ar de glory-
 crown?
Who's a gwine fer ter stan' stiff-kneed en bol'.
En answer to der name at de callin' er de roll?
  You better come now ef you comin'—
  Ole Satun is loose en a bummin'—
  De wheels er distruckshun is a hummin'—
  Oh, come 'long, sinner, ef you comin'!

De song er salvashun is a mighty sweet song,
En de Pairidise win' blow fur en blow strong,
En Aberham's bosom, hit's saft en hit's wide,
En right dar's de place whar de sinners oughter hide!
   Oh, you nee'nter be a stoppin' en a lookin';
   Ef you fool wid ole Satun you'll git took in;
   You'll hang on de aidge en get shook in,
   Ef you keep on a stoppin' en a lookin'.

De time is right now, en dish yer's de place—
Let de sun er salvashun shine squar' in yo' face;
Fight de battles er de Lord, fight soon en fight late,
En you'll allers fine a latch ter de golden gate.
   No use fer ter wait twel ter-morrer,
   De sun musn't set on yo' sorrer—
   Sin's ez sharp ez a bamboo-brier,
   Ax de Lord fer ter fetch you up higher!

II.

CAMP-MEETING SONG.*

Oh, de worril is roun' en de worril is wide—
 Lord! 'member deze chillun in de mornin'—

---

* In the days of slavery, the religious services held by the negroes who accompanied their owners to the camp-meetings were marvels of earnestness and devotion.

Hit's a mighty long ways up de mountain side,
 En dey ain't no place fer dem sinners fer ter hide,
 En dey ain't no place whar sin kin abide,
  W'en de Lord shill come in de mornin'!
   Look up en look aroun',
   Fling yo' burden on de groun',
  Hit's a gittin' mighty close on ter mornin'!
   Smoove away sin's frown—
   Retch up en git de crown,
  W'at de Lord will fetch in de mornin'!

De han' er ridem'shun, hit's hilt out ter you—
 Lord! 'member dem sinners in de mornin'!
Hit's a mighty pashent han', but de days is but few,
W'en Satun, he'll come a demandin' un his due,
En de stiff-neck sinners 'll be smotin' all fru—
 Oh, you better git ready fer de mornin'!
   Look up en set yo' face
   Todes de green hills er grace
  'Fo' de sun rises up in de mornin'—
   Oh, you better change yo' base,
   Hits yo' soul's las' race
  Fer de glory dat's a comin' in de mornin'!

De farmer gits ready w'en de lan's all plowed
 Fer ter sow dem seeds in de mornin'—
De sperrit may be puny en de flesh may be proud,
But you better cut loose fum de scoffin' crowd,

En jine dese Christuns w'at's a cryin' out loud
  Fer de Lord fer ter come in de mornin'!
    Shout loud en shout long,
    Let de ekkoes ans'er strong,
  W'en de sun rises up in de mornin'!
    Oh, you allers will be wrong
    Twel you choose ter belong
  Ter de Marster w'at's a comin' in de mornin'!

III.

CORN-SHUCKING SONG.

Oh, de fus news you know de day'll be a breakin'—
  (Hey O! Hi O! Up'n down de Bango! *)
An' de fier be a burnin' en' de ash-cake a bakin',
  (Hey O! Hi O! Up'n down de Bango!)
An' de hen'll be a hollerin' en de boss 'll be a wakin'—
  (Hey O! Hi O! Up'n down de Bango!)
Better git up, nigger, en give yo'se'f a shakin'—
  (Hi O, Miss Sindy Ann!)

Oh, honey! w'en you see dem ripe stars a fallin'—
  (Hey O! Hi O! Up'n down de Bango!)

---

* So far as I know, "Bango" is a meaningless term, introduced
on account of its sonorous ruggedness.

Oh, honey! w'en you year de rain-crow a callin'—
    (Hey O! Hi O! Up'n down de Bango!)
Oh, honey! w'en you year dat red calf a bawlin'—
    (Hey O! Hi O! Up'n down de Bango!)
Den de day time's comin', a creepin' en a crawlin'—
    (Hi O, Miss Sindy Ann!)

Fer de los' ell en yard * is a huntin' fer de mornin',
    (Hi O! git 'long! go 'way!)
En she'll ketch up widdus 'fo' we ever git dis corn in—
    (Oh, go 'way, Sindy Ann!)

Oh, honey! w'en you year dat tin horn a tootin'—
    (Hey O! Hi O! Up'n down de Bango!)
Oh, honey, w'en you year de squinch owl a hootin'—
    (Hey O! Hi O! Up'n down de Bango!)
Oh, honey! w'en you year dem little pigs a rootin'—
    (Hey O! Hi O! Up'n down de Bango!)
Right den she's a comin' a skippin' en a scootin'—
    (Hi O, Miss Sindy Ann!)

Oh, honey, w'en you year dat roan mule whicker—
    (Hey O! Hi O! Up'n down de Bango!)
W'en you see Mister Moon turnin' pale en gittin'
    sicker—
    (Hey O! Hi O! Up'n down de Bango!)

---

* The sword and belt in the constellation of Orion.

Den hit's time fer ter handle dat corn a little quicker—
  (Hey O ! Hi O ! Up'n down de Bango !)
Ef you wanter git a smell er old Marster's jug er
    licker—
  (Hi O, Miss Sindy Ann !)

Fer de los' ell en yard is a huntin' fer de mornin'
  (Hi O ! git 'long ! go 'way !)
En she'll ketch up widdus 'fo' we ever git dis corn in—
  (Oh, go 'way, Sindy Ann !)
You niggers 'cross dar ! you better stop your dancin'—
  (Hey O ! Hi O ! Up'n down de Bango !)
No use fer ter come a flingin' un yo' "sha'n'ts" in—
  (Hey O ! Hi O ! Up'n down de Bango !)
No use fer ter come a flingin' un yo' "can't's" in—
  (Hey O ! Hi O ! Up'n down de Bango !)
Kaze dey ain't no time fer yo' pattin' ner yo' prancin' !
  (Hi O, Miss Sindy Ann !)

Mr. Rabbit see de Fox, en he sass um en jaws um—
  (Hey O ! Hi O ! Up'n down de Bango !)
Mr. Fox ketch de Rabbit, en he scratch um en he
    claws um—
  (Hey O ! Hi O ! Up'n down de Bango !)
En he tar off de hide, en he chaws um en he
    gnyaws um—
  (Hey O ! Hi O ! Up'n down de Bango !)
Same like gal chawin' sweet gum en rozzum—
  (Hi O, Miss Sindy Ann !)

Fer de los' ell en yard is a huntin' fer de mornin'
    (Hi O! git 'long! go 'way!)
En she'll ketch up widdus 'fo' we ever git dis corn in—
    (Oh, go 'way, Sindy Ann!)

Oh, work on, boys! give deze shucks a mighty
       wringin'—
    (Hey O! Hi O! Up'n down de Bango!)
'Fo' de boss come aroun' a dangin' en a dingin'—
    (Hey O! Hi O! Up'n down de Bango!)

Git up en move aroun'! set dem big han's ter swingin'—
    (Hey O! Hi O! Up'n down de Bango!)
Git up'n shout loud! let de w'ite folks year you singin'!
    (Hi O, Miss Sindy Ann!)

Fer de los' ell en yard is a huntin' fer de mornin'
    (Hi O! git 'long! go 'way!)
En she'll ketch up widdus 'fo' we ever git dis corn in.
    (Oh, go 'way Sindy Ann!)

IV.

THE PLOUGH-HANDS' SONG.

(Jasper County—1860.)

Nigger mighty happy w'en he layin' by co'n—
  Dat sun's a slantin' ;
Nigger mighty happy w'en he year de dinner-ho'n—
  Dat sun's a slantin' ;
En he mo' happy still w'en de night draws on—
  Dat sun's a slantin' ;
Dat sun's a slantin' des ez sho's you bo'n !
  En it's rise up, Primus ! fetch anudder yell :
  Dat ole dun cow's des a shakin' up 'er bell,
  En de frogs chunin' up 'fo' de jew done fell :
  Good-night, Mr. Killdee ! I wish you mighty well !
   —Mr. Killdee ! I wish you mighty well !
    —I wish you mighty well !

De co'n 'll be ready 'g'inst dumplin day—
  Dat sun's a slantin' ;
But nigger gotter watch, en stick, en stay—
  Dat sun's a slantin' ;
Same ez de bee-martin watchin' un de jay—
  Dat sun's a slantin' ;
Dat sun's a slantin' en a slippin' away !
  Den it's rise up, Primus ! en gin it t'um strong ;
  De cow's gwine home wid der ding-dang-dong—

Sling in anudder tetch er de ole-time song :
Good-night, Mr. Whipperwill! don't stay long!
—Mr. Whipperwill! don't stay long!
—Don't stay long!

V.

CHRISTMAS PLAY-SONG.

(MYRICK PLACE, PUTNAM COUNTY—1858.)

HI my rinktum !   Black gal sweet,
Same like goodies w'at de w'ite folks eat ;
Ho my Riley ! don't you take'n tell 'er name,
En den ef sumpin' happen you won't ketch de blame ;
Hi my rinktum ! better take'n hide yo' plum ;
Joree don't holler eve'y time he fine a wum.

Den it's hi my rinktum !
Don't git no udder man ;
En it's ho my Riley !
Fetch out Miss Dilsey Ann !

Ho my Riley !   Yaller gal fine ;
She may be yone but she oughter be mine !
Hi my rinktum !   Lemme git by,
En see w'at she mean by de cut er dat eye !
Ho my Riley ! better shet dat do'—
De w'ite folks 'll b'leeve we er t'arin up de flo'.

Den it's ho my Riley !
   Come a siftin' up ter me !
En it's hi my rinktum !
   Dis de way ter twis' yo' knee !

Hi my rinktum !   Ain't de eas' gittin' red ?
De squinch owl shiver like he wanter go ter bed ;
Ho my Riley ! but de gals en de boys,
Des now gittin' so dey kin sorter make a noise.
Hi my rinktum ! let de yaller gal 'lone ;
Niggers don't hanker arter sody in de pone.
   Den it's hi my rinktum !
   Better try anudder plan ;
   An' it's ho my Riley !
   Trot out Miss Dilsey Ann !

Ho my Riley !   In de happy Chrismus' time
De niggers shake der cloze a huntin' fer a dime.
Hi my rinktum !   En den dey shake der feet,
En greaze derse'f wid de good ham meat.
Ho my Riley ! dev eat en dey cram,
En bimeby ole Miss 'll be a sendin' out de dram.
   Den it's ho my Riley !
   You hear dat, Sam !
   En it's hi my rinktum !
   Be a sendin' out de dram !

VI.

PLANTATION PLAY-SONG.

(Putnam County—1856.)

Hit's a gittin' mighty late, w'en de Guinny-hins squall,
En you better dance now, ef you gwineter dance a tall,
Fer by dis time ter-morrer night you can't hardly crawl,
Kaze you'll hatter take de hoe ag'in en likewise de
    maul—
Don't you hear dat bay colt a kickin' in his stall?
Stop yo' humpin' up
  yo' sho'lders—
    Dat'll never do!
Hop light, ladies,
    Oh, Miss Loo!
Hit takes a heap er
  scrougin'
    Fer ter git you
    thoo—
Hop light, ladies,
    Oh, Miss Loo!

Ef you niggers don't watch, you'll sing anudder
    chune,
Fer de sun'll rise'n ketch you ef you don't be mighty
    soon;
En de stars is gittin' paler, en de ole gray coon
Is a settin' in de grape-vine a watchin' fer de moon.

W'en a feller comes a knockin'
  Des holler—*Oh, shoo!*
Hop light, ladies,
  Oh, Miss Loo!
Oh, swing dat yaller gal!
  Do, boys, do!
Hop light, ladies,
  Oh, Miss Loo!

Oh, tu'n me loose! Lemme 'lone! Go way, now!
W'at you speck I come a dancin' fer ef I dunno how?
Deze de ve'y kinder footses w'at kicks up a row;
Can't you jump inter de middle en make yo' gal a bow?
  Look at dat merlatter man
    A follerin' up Sue;
  Hop light, ladies,
    Oh, Miss Loo!
  De boys ain't a gwine
    W'en you cry *boo hoo*—
  Hop light, ladies,
    Oh, Miss Loo!

VII.

TRANSCRIPTIONS.[*]

1. A PLANTATION CHANT.

HIT's eighteen hunder'd forty-en-fo',
Christ done open dat He'v'mly do'—
    An' I don't wanter stay yer no longer;
Hit's eighteen hunder'd forty-en-five,
Christ done made dat dead man alive—
    An' I don't wanter stay yer no longer.
      You ax me ter run home,
        Little childun—
      Run home, dat sun done roll—
        An' I don't wanter stay yer no longer.

Hit's eighteen hunder'd forty-en-six,
Christ is got us a place done fix—
    An' I don't wanter stay yer no longer;
Hit's eighteen hunder'd forty-en-sev'm
Christ done sot a table in Hev'm—
    An' I don't wanter stay yer no longer.

---

[*] If these are adaptations from songs the negroes have caught from the whites, their origin is very remote. I have transcribed them literally, and I regard them as in the highest degree characteristic.

28

You ax me ter run home,
Little childun—
Run home, dat sun done roll—
An' I don't wanter stay yer no longer.

Hit's eighteen hunder'd forty-en-eight,
Christ done make dat crooked way straight—
An' I don't wanter stay yer no longer;
Hit's eighteen hunder'd forty-en-nine,
Christ done tv'n dat water inter wine—
An' I don't wanter stay yer no longer.
You ax me ter run home,
Little childun—
Run home, dat sun done roll—
An' I don't wanter stay yer no longer.

Hit's eighteen hunder'd forty-en-ten,
Christ is de mo'ner's onliest fr'en'—
An' I don't wanter stay yer no longer;
Hit's eighteen hunder'd forty-en-'lev'm,
Christ'll be at de do' w'en we all git ter Hev'm—
An' I don't wanter stay yer no longer.
You ax me ter run home,
Little childun—
Run home, dat sun done roll—
An' I don't wanter stay yer no longer.

2. A Plantation Serenade.

De ole bee make de honey-comb,
  De young bee make de honey,
De niggers make de cotton en
    co'n,
  En de w'ite folks gits de
    money.

De raccoon he's a cu'us man,
  He never walk twel dark,
En nuthin' never 'sturbs his mine,
  Twel he hear ole Bringer bark.

    De raccoon totes a bushy tail,
      De 'possum totes no ha'r,
    Mr. Rabbit, he come skippin' by,
      He ain't got none ter spar'.

    Monday mornin' break er day,
      W'ite folks got me gwine,
    But Sat'dy night, w'en de sun goes down,
      Dat yaller gal's in my mine.

    Fifteen poun' er meat a week,
      W'isky fer ter sell,
    Oh, how can a young man stay at home,
      Dem gals dey look so well?

Met a 'possum in de road—
Brer 'Possum, whar you gwine?
I thank my stars, I bless my life,
I'm a huntin' fer de muscadine.

VIII.

THE BIG BETHEL CHURCH.

DE Big Bethel chu'ch! de Big Bethel chu'ch!
  Done put ole Satun behine um;
Ef a sinner git loose fum enny udder chu'ch,
  De Big Bethel chu'ch will fine um!

Hit's good ter be dere, en it's sweet ter be dere,
  Wid de sisterin' all aroun' you—
A shakin' dem shackles er mussy en' love
  Wharwid de Lord is boun' you.

Hit's sweet ter be dere en lissen ter de hymes,
  En hear dem mo'ners a shoutin'—
Dey done reach de place whar der ain't no room
  Fer enny mo' weepin' en doubtin'.

Hit's good ter be dere w'en de sinners all jine
  Wid de brudderin in dere singin',
En it look like Gaberl gwine ter rack up en blow
  En set dem heav'm bells ter ringin'!

Oh, de Big Bethel chu'ch! de Big Bethel chu'ch,
　　Done put ole Satun behine um;
Ef a sinner git loose fum enny udder chu'ch
　　De Big Bethel chu'ch will fine um!

IX.

TIME GOES BY TURNS.

Dar's a pow'ful rassle 'twix de Good en de Bad,
　　En de Bad's got de all-under holt;
En w'en de wuss come, she come i'on-clad,
　　En you hatter hole yo' bref fer de jolt.

But des todes de las' Good gits de knee-lock,
　　En dey draps ter de groun'—*ker flop!*
Good had de inturn, en he stan' like a rock,
　　En he bleedzd fer ter be on top.

De dry wedder breaks wid a big thunder-clap,
　　Fer dey ain't no drout' w'at kin las',
But de seasons w'at whoops up de cotton crap,
　　Likewise dey freshens up de grass.

De rain fall so saf' in de long dark night,
　　Twel you hatter hole yo' han' fer a sign,
But de drizzle w'at sets de tater-slips right
　　Is de makin' er de May-pop vine.

In de mellerest groun' de clay root'll ketch
　　En hole ter de tongue er de plow,
En a pine-pole gate at de gyardin-patch
　　Never'll keep out de ole brindle cow.

One en all on us knows who's a pullin' at de bits
　　Like de lead-mule dat g'ides by de rein,
En yit, somehow er nudder, de bestest un us gits
　　Mighty sick er de tuggin' at de chain.

Hump yo'se'f ter de load en fergit de distress,
　　En dem w'at stan's by ter scoff,
Fer de harder de pullin', de longer de res',
　　En de bigger de feed in de troff.